S0-BZO-275

Date: 2/16/22

GRA TOUYA V.1
Touya,
A tale of the secret saint.

PALM BEACH COUNTY
LIBRARY SYSTEM
3650 Summit Boulevard
West Palm Beach, FL 33406-4198

CONTENTS

A Tale of the Secret Saint

NOVEL

1

WRITTEN BY
Touya

ILLUSTRATED BY
chibi

Airship

Seven Seas Entertainment

Tensei Sita Daiseijyo ha, Seijyo dearuko towohitakakusu Vol.1
© Touya, chibi 2019
Originally published in Japan in 2019
by EARTH STAR Entertainment, Tokyo.
English translation rights arranged
with EARTH STAR Entertainment, Tokyo,
through TOHAN CORPORATION, Tokyo.

No portion of this book may be reproduced or transmitted
in any form without written permission from the copyright
holders. This is a work of fiction. Names, characters, places,
and incidents are the products of the author's imagination
or are used fictitiously. Any resemblance to actual events,
locales, or persons, living or dead, is entirely coincidental.
Any information or opinions expressed by the creators of this
book belong to those individual creators and do not necessarily
reflect the views of Seven Seas Entertainment or its employees.

Seven Seas press and purchase enquiries can be sent to
Marketing Manager Lianne Sentar at press@gomanga.com.
Information regarding the distribution and purchase of
digital editions is available from Digital Manager CK Russell
at digital@gomanga.com.

Seven Seas and the Seven Seas logo are trademarks of
Seven Seas Entertainment. All rights reserved.

Follow Seven Seas Entertainment online at
sevenseasentertainment.com.

TRANSLATION: Kevin Ishizaka
ADAPTATION: Matthew Birkenhauer
COVER DESIGN: Hanase Qi
LOGO DESIGN: George Panella
INTERIOR LAYOUT & DESIGN: Clay Gardner
COPY EDITOR: Jade Gardner
PROOFREADER: Meg van Huygen
LIGHT NOVEL EDITOR: Rebecca Scoble
PREPRESS TECHNICIAN: Rhiannon Rasmussen-Silverstein
PRODUCTION MANAGER: Lissa Pattillo
MANAGING EDITOR: Julie Davis
ASSOCIATE PUBLISHER: Adam Arnold
PUBLISHER: Jason DeAngelis

ISBN: 978-1-64827-646-0
Printed in Canada
First Printing: October 2021
10 9 8 7 6 5 4 3 2 1

Prologue

THEY SAY YOUR LIFE flashes before your eyes when you die.
Fifteen years, huh? I thought. *It's a bit on the short side, but I guess...when your time's up, it's up. I wonder what's going to flash before my eyes? What will I remember? What will I...I...huh? Wh—?*

Strangely enough, I didn't see memories of my own lost life at all, but of the life I had before...

Memories belonging to the Great Saint who could heal fatal wounds in the blink of an eye while strengthening her allies to absurd levels of power.

Memories belonging to the Great Saint who could ward off all attacks—be they physical or magical.

Memories belonging to the Great Saint, showing power far beyond anything passed down in nursery tales.

"This is insane, this can't be true..." I coughed up blood as I cried out. "This kind of power...it would turn the world upside down."

Bleeding out from the wounds left by a monster's attack, the memories of my past life rushed back to me in my final moments...

"She'll die if she attempts the coming-of-age ceremony!" My older sister's exasperated voice echoed throughout the room.

My father and all four of us siblings had gathered in the biggest room of our estate to discuss whether I should attempt the dangerous coming-of-age ceremony that all knights must pass to finish their training.

My older brother looked at me as he spoke: "I hear she's improved a bit, though. She's gotta have at least a fifty percent chance of survival, right?"

The veins on my sister's forehead bulged as she glared at my brother. "Which makes the death of our sister a *coin toss*. This family already has four knights; we don't need any more!"

My brother and sister glared at each other while my eldest brother—sitting across from me—polished his sword, completely uninterested.

My father watched quietly with his arms folded before deliberately looking over my way. "What do *you* want to do, Fia?"

"Huh? O-oh, I-I'll do ithbfft!" Ack, I'd bit my tongue. I'd just gotten so flustered to hear someone call my name for the first time in forever.

My sister gave me a pleading look. "Fia…you don't have to become a knight. Father is vice-captain of a knight brigade. Your brothers and I are knights; our family is secure. You can choose any profession you like."

"If it's my choice," I said, looking my sister square in the eyes, "then I still want to become a knight." It was my decision. It had been my dream since I was little. Surely she could understand that...

My sister fell silent. After a while, she let out a heavy, defeated sigh. "I...I know. Goodness knows, I've seen you training enough for it since you were a kid. You admire them so much... Well, fine. Go through with the ceremony. But if you're not back within the day, I'm coming to look for you!"

And so it was decided: I would perform the coming-of-age ceremony the following day.

A Tale of the
Secret
Saint

1
The Path to Knighthood

I AM FIA RUUD, youngest of the Ruud family.

People always told me that I took after my beautiful mother, with my red hair and golden eyes. Odd, isn't it? They'd compliment her, but they never called *me* beautiful.

That wasn't the only thing I inherited from my mother, however. Her frame was small, she couldn't gain muscle mass, couldn't...well, even develop much of a chest. No training could fix that. That's a problem if you want to be a knight.

Knights can own a domain, you see. Someone knighted by the king immediately becomes the head of their family, and the status of that family rises nearly to the level of nobility. But if that head dies and there is no knight to succeed them, the family in question is stripped of their status.

And so the children of knights all work hard to become knights themselves, including me. I'd longed to be a knight ever since I was young, even if it was an extremely difficult path.

Being the kingdom's most prestigious profession, the pass rate for the knight's exam was astonishingly low. The odds ranged from one in fifty to one in a hundred.

Knighthood was the most respected position in the kingdom, as it was given by the kingdom itself. Massive wealth came with the job, although not without good reason. Being a knight meant, after all, that you had a duty to protect the Royal Castle, its royalty, and the kingdom itself. Those duties branched off from there—from maintaining order within the kingdom, to patrolling the border, to dealing with the ever-rising tide of monsters, a knight's work was never done.

I knew, being from a family of knights, that sword skill was the most vital talent for anyone hoping for knighthood. I'd polished my swordsmanship from a young age, and I never lacked for sparring partners. There were, after all, many knights in our domain, including my own siblings.

Eat, sleep, practice, repeat. For years I ran through this cycle. It was tough but fulfilling work...until I realized something.

I hadn't won a single practice match. Not one.

In fact...I'd even lost to the newbie who'd started practicing only three months prior.

In *fact,* I'd time a step-in perfectly, and somehow *my* sword would be the one sent flying.

Why? Well...I didn't have much talent for the sword.

Surely hard work will make up for my lack of natural talent, I told myself. *I'm not trying to become the best knight in the world or anything. Just being a rank-and-file knight would be enough for me...*

It might've been because knighthood was my dream, or simple stubbornness, but I was willing to do whatever it took to become a knight. My lack of talent didn't discourage me from training. I eventually became just barely strong enough to enter a knight brigade—or at least, I thought so.

During that time, my siblings—blessed by their natural gifts—became knights and left the estate. Only my sister's departure moved me; my brothers had ignored me after discovering I had no talent for the sword, so their absence meant little. As for my father, he discovered my ineptitude long before my brothers did. He'd been the first to pretend that I didn't exist.

When he left to protect the western territories as the vice-captain of the Fourteenth Knight Brigade, I hardly noticed his absence.

So you see, that's why opinions were divided as to whether or not I should go forward with the coming-of-age ceremony. My brothers, my father, my sister—they'd all been away, and none of them knew how much I had improved...or if I'd improved at all.

The coming-of-age ceremony itself was simple. When you turned fifteen, you'd pick up a stone, any stone, from anywhere. You'd then take that stone and show it to a diviner who would tell your fortune using the stone's shape and color.

But my family had a special twist on that. Nothing changed if the person coming of age didn't want to become a knight; but if they did, they'd have to hunt a monster for the magic stone inside. That would prove their strength.

Monsters are powerful, magical creatures that carry magic stones in their bodies. The stones vary in size depending on the strength of the creature. Many monsters inhabited the depths of the forest, so my sister tried to discourage me from becoming a knight at all. She wanted me to give up on it and simply get a normal stone.

The younger of my two brothers, on the other hand, said I had an obligation as the daughter of a knight to go after a magic stone, even if it killed me. My oldest brother simply didn't care. As for my father, he left the decision to me—he didn't care either.

What other choice could I make? If I wanted to become a knight, I had to collect a magic stone. So that's what I would do.

The Coming-of-Age Ceremony

I WOKE UP EARLY the next morning and quickly washed my face, drank a cup of water, and got ready to leave. I didn't have the appetite for breakfast. Too nervous.

To my surprise, my sister was waiting for me at the door. She didn't say anything and simply handed me a small vial.

Oria Ruud was her name, second child of the Ruud family and my older sister. She was absolutely beautiful, with dark-brown hair that came down to her chest when not tied back. She wasn't afraid to look anyone straight in the eyes, either, which sent men's hearts racing—her eyes were as stunning as everything else about her.

The vial she handed me contained a clear, sparkling liquid. Just one look and I knew full well how valuable this item was. "Oria..." What could I even say? "For me?"

"Yes, for you. Let me be very clear: if you get hurt, you are to drink this and immediately run away. Do you understand?!" She made no attempt to hide her worry.

The vial was a healing potion, a special kind of mixture that couldn't be made by a mere pharmacist. Only the healing magic of a saint could create such a thing, and saints were few and far between. A saint only had enough magic to make a few healing potions a day...so my sister must have paid an exorbitant amount of money for this.

"Healing potions aren't perfect," she continued. "It won't heal serious injuries or lost limbs, so don't let it make you reckless. Better to avoid getting hurt at all, okay? You hear me?!"

"Oria...thank you." I took her hand in mine, grasping the vial. Her hands were calloused. Knight's hands, proof that she'd devoted herself to protecting the people. But despite all that, she still found time to care about me.

I swore to myself I would repay her kindness in full by bringing home the largest magic stone I could.

"Fia, you're getting that odd look in your eyes, and I *know* you're thinking something outrageous, so listen up: a magic stone is a magic stone, no matter the size. Bring back the smallest one you can!"

I swore to myself I would repay her bluntness in full by bringing home the smallest magic stone I could.

That being said, the odds of encountering any monsters at all weren't high. Adventurers regularly cleared the areas near towns and villages of monsters, after all. If you wanted to find one, you had to venture deep into the forest.

For starters, I'd take a look around the forest of my family's domain. Let's see...there were certainly a lot of bugs around, a few rabbits or foxes, but no monsters.

A One-Eyed Rat would be the best monster to target—small and weak, I thought to myself. *Perhaps I can find one alone, looking for food. Maybe in a cave somewhere? There should be a cave in the eastern part of the woods.*

Surprised by my own calmness, I found myself heading east through the forest. Perhaps I *could* do this. I'd trained with the sword on a daily basis, after all; one of my friends even said I'd improved a lot this past year. Surely I could handle just one monster by now.

I've got to have confidence. I can do this. I can do this! I carefully monitored my surroundings, repeating those little affirmations in my head all the while.

I must've walked for an hour or so before I finally noticed something was off. The forest was quiet. Much too quiet. When had I last seen an animal? When had I last *heard* an animal?

A full-body shiver ran through me like a winter wind. Something wasn't right. I took a step back, ready to flee...

And a small whine reached my ears.

I should leave. That would be the wise thing, wouldn't it? Knowing that in my bones, I still found myself drawing closer to the source of that miserable whine—a bloodied chick at the base of a tree.

It couldn't have been more than a few days old. Its small, black, curled-up body bled onto the dirt, and it took shallow, pained breaths with its tiny eyes clamped shut. It wouldn't last half a day, for sure. And yet, for some strange reason, that lingering chill from before vanished without a trace the moment I laid eyes on it.

Was there something special about this chick? *Should I save it? Should I run?*

The chick opened its eyes slightly. Those blue eyes, boundless like the clear sky, seemed to plead to me.

My hands moved without thinking. I fed it the healing potion my sister gave me. I stroked its body as I whispered to it, telling it that it would be okay. Just when I thought it had stabilized, it gave a loud shriek.

It must've been in pain—yes, that was it! Healing potions forcibly speed up the user's natural recovery, and the pain from that is intense.

"It'll be—" *Okay* is what I started to say when the chick began to grow before my eyes.

And grow. And grow still more till it was many times my size. It bellowed.

Then, effortlessly, it sank its teeth into me.

And it tore out my shoulder.

Oh...of course. My consciousness was fading, and all I could do was feel like a fool. There were no birds in this world with black feathers. The only black winged creature was the legendary and dangerous black dragon, said to be stronger than a hundred knights. It had to have been fatally injured.

The black dragon must've transformed itself into an infant to trick me, and I'd fallen for it—I healed it, and now...

Now everything dimmed. I could feel my blood pouring out. The black dragon opened its mouth again.

This is it, I thought. *All my training was pointless. I was never more than a frog trapped in a well, its whole world a few stone walls.*

They say your life flashes before your eyes when you die.

Fifteen years, huh? I thought. *It's a bit on the short side, but I guess...when your time's up, it's up. I wonder what's going to flash before my eyes? What will I remember? What will I...I...huh? Wh—?*

The black dragon bit into my side. My vision went red from the tearing pain.

That was when the strangest thing occurred. Memories of a life other than mine surfaced to my mind—memories of my previous life as the Great Saint, with power that far surpassed even the wildest nursery tales.

"This is insane, this can't be true..." I coughed up blood as I cried out. "This kind of power...it would turn the world upside down..."

Bleeding out, the dragon's teeth sinking into my side, the memories of my past life came flooding back.

A Tale of the
Secret Saint

3

Saints

THE NÁV KINGDOM was my home, and it was one of two great powers on the continent. This kingdom was founded by the Great Saint, and the royal family was said to be descended directly from her.

The legends told that the Great Saint and a brave hero worked to seal away a demon lord who terrorized the world. In time, the two married. Their descendants would rule the kingdom peacefully for generations.

The legends were lies.

Saints are women with the power to heal. Whether it's healing a wound instantaneously, regrowing limbs, even curing illness—all of those things were once easily within the power of a saint. But over the centuries, the power and number of saints dwindled. Once numerous, the saints became a rarity.

The royal family and the nobles noticed and did anything they could to marry saints and pass down their powers to the next generations—saint powers were more likely to be passed down to the next generation than most forms of magic. The kingdom had been founded through the grace of the saints, after all, and its continual peace relied on their existence.

Healing magic was vital in battle, of course, and the power of a saint could make all the difference between victory and defeat. Sure, you could use a healing potion...but those took time to work, requiring a momentary retreat from the front. Saints were much faster than any potion.

Saints alone could use that incredible power...and still, their numbers kept on dwindling. People kept being born with attack magic, but those with healing magic petered out. The kingdom took custody of any newborn saints. All girls underwent mandatory testing at a young age to check for that power. Any saints discovered were immediately taken to the church, where they were taught how to use their power. Those girls were then married off to nobles at a young age, which sometimes let those of common birth rise in station.

All saints spent their days working for the kingdom, making healing potions and assisting knights on expeditions. In turn, those knights protected and served them. A saint acting as an adventurer would be, of course, out of the question.

The saints came to be worshiped throughout the kingdom, given the highest honor and best treatment. Their age didn't matter, nor did their origin. And so, worshiped by all, the saints themselves grew conceited.

They began to believe themselves to be the chosen ones.

4
The Great Saint

I N MY PAST LIFE, I was known as a "Great Saint." It was a title of honor, granted to saints with the power to *instantly* heal all injuries, restore lost limbs, and cure nearly any illness imaginable. And for that entire lifetime, I was the only one to attain that title.

While I garnered respect as the Great Saint, the same could not be said for other saints. There were simply too many of us. Back then, more than half of all women were saints.

Unlike attack magic, healing magic required a pact with the spirits—and those spirits made pacts freely. Why? Well, ancient legends of the kingdom's founding told of a figure known as the Spirit Lord. This Spirit Lord fell in love with a human girl, and their child became the ancestor of the royal family.

And so the spirits loved the kingdom and made pacts with its women. Humans and spirits lived in harmony; the humans loved, honored, and respected the spirits. In return, spirits lent power to the saints.

In my past life—my life as the Great Saint—I was the royal princess. As royalty, I could draw far more power from the spirits than others. Playing in the mountains and forests, I grew close to the spirits. People believed that they couldn't speak, yet I heard their voices. And from their voices I learned the power of a saint: the power to heal and regrow limbs, to cure illnesses and brew healing potions for light wounds.

And that was only the beginning. They taught me the power to cure ailments like paralyzed limbs or a charmed mind; granted me the power to improve the speed and strength of a human body; taught me protection magics to ward off physical and magical attacks; showed me how to imbue magic properties into equipment; and finally, taught me the power to bottle all of these incredible abilities into potions.

After mastering these powers, I received the rare title of Great Saint...but there was no time to rest. A great demon lord threatened humanity, so I journeyed with my older brothers—the princes—to defeat him.

After an arduous battle, we succeeded in sealing the demon lord away...but I had no magic left in me after the fight. To use healing magic, you must combine your own magical power with the strength granted by the spirits.

I couldn't use my power, and my brothers abandoned me.

"Look at you. What an eyesore. So full of yourself, just because they call you the Great Saint!" yelled my oldest brother, the first prince.

"Ha ha! Don't you know you're expendable? The kingdom is

full of saints like you, all just as worthless," laughed the second prince.

"Sorry, no triumphant return home for you," the third prince snarled. "No, you're going to be ripped to shreds by the demons here. In fact, you being a woman, I bet some really disgusting demons will have their way with you before they kill you. We're the ones who bear the injuries and fight! All you do is stand in the back and cast magic. You deserve to die here."

I could do nothing but lie there—magic expended, body drenched in sweat, heart pounding, fingers too heavy to even lift.

My three brothers, my *own family*, drank the advanced healing potions I'd given them earlier...and threw the empty vials down beside me. When they left, they did not look back.

I have to hide... I'd thought. I didn't want to think what the demons would do to me, the one who sealed away their ruler. *If I can just hide for a bit, I can recover some magic and heal myself, then maybe find a way out.*

Those thoughts and more raced through my head as I crawled forward...and a foot stepped down on my hand. Despairing, I looked up to see a handsome demon gazing down on me. Demons hold beauty in proportion to their strength...and so, of course, my fate was now sealed.

I recognized the demon too; they called him the right hand of the demon lord.

He toyed with me, tormented me, taking due care not to let me die quickly. I was bound. He carved demon writing all over my skin, laughed scornfully, and hurled abuse as I struggled to break free.

"This is happening to you because you're a saint."

He despised the saint who'd sealed the demon lord away, so he reminded me, over and over, why he was torturing me. He seemed to love saying it.

"You're toyed with because you're a saint."

"You're tormented because you're a saint."

"You're humiliated because you're a saint."

His words seeped into me like poison as he rained his cruelty down on me. I'd long since lost my grasp on time before I fully understood what he was telling me.

All of this was happening because I was a saint.

I was toyed with because I was a saint.

Tormented because I was a saint.

Humiliated because I was a saint.

And I'd be killed because I was a saint.

Only then did the demon finally kill me.

5

Awakening

I T HURT TO BREATHE. My throat, my lungs, my organs—everything burned. I coughed up blood with each breath.

The burning, the aching, the pain—I just wanted it to *stop*.

Just as that thought crossed my mind, the pain suddenly started to fade. Breathing grew easier. My consciousness returned. I could feel the wind brush my cheek and the sun warming me. I could smell the forest around me.

Huh? What was I doing? I sat up...and came face-to-face with a black dragon, drenched in blood, staring right at me.

I screamed, naturally. *"Eeeeek!"* Staggering, I managed to stand up and draw my sword. "S-s-s-s-s-stay away or I'll c-c-c-c-cut you!" I stuttered out.

The black dragon looked at me in puzzlement. **"'S-s-s-s-s-stay'? 'C-c-c-c-cut'? I haven't heard those words before."**

Was the creature mocking me or genuinely asking?

Oh, right, it had just torn me to shreds—the memory of

being viciously attacked by this dragon came rushing back. "Ah, my, my arm! My side! I'm bleeding out!"

Panicked, I touched my body and...found it intact. I *had* been injured...hadn't I?

At that, the black dragon looked down at its great feet and said, "**I'm sorry. I mistook the pain from your healing potion for an attack and bit you...and despite that, you still saved me with your healing magic. Thank you.**"

"Um...huh?" Healing magic? From me? I wasn't a saint, was I? That had been a dream. It *had* to be a dream. "*Mmm*, I don't get it. I'm going home. Home. Then...sleep. No point thinking about it right now."

My legs gave out, and I flopped back down onto the ground. Suddenly I wondered if I had enough energy to go anywhere.

But then I looked back at the dragon and shot right back up. Was it going to attack? It...didn't *look* like it wanted to attack. That was enough for me; completely wiped out, I decided to lie down. "I think I'll just sleep here... Good night."

The dragon spoke as I closed my eyes. "**It appears that you're experiencing magic fatigue. Unsurprising; you used the advanced spell 'Full Heal.' I'd give you some of my magic if I could, but—**"

The voice grew distant. I started slipping into sleep when I felt someone shake my shoulder.

"**Miss, please don't fall asleep yet. We dragons devote our lives to those who save us. I am forever in your service.**"

"*Mmh...*"

"Why don't I form a pact of servitude with you? That way I can share my magic. What's your name?"

"My...name? Fia Ruud."

"My deepest thanks. I, Zavilia, Black Dragon King, offer my blood, my body, and my soul in eternal servitude to my master, Fia Ruud."

Through closed eyelids, I saw light.

"*Heh.* With this, I am yours. Many monsters will appear tonight, drawn in by the alluring scent of saint blood. Knowing this, you still manage to sleep peacefully. How surprising."

Something warm and calming flowed into my body. Lethargy overwhelmed me. I thought I heard the black dragon say something else, but I couldn't make it out before drifting off...

When I woke, it was morning. I must have slept for quite some time; my head felt clear and my body rested. I tried to roll over, and...I felt something smooth covering me. Had my bed always felt like this?

I reached out to feel it. In response, my bed reached out to touch my hand...? Curious, I slowly opened my eyes to see two blue pupils staring at me.

"Black dragon!" I stood up at once. I really had spent an entire night in the forest, and yet I didn't feel cold. I felt perfectly rested, in fact.

"I wasn't cold at all," I wondered aloud. "Did you keep me warm throughout the night?"

"Of course. It's my duty to protect my master." The monster seemed truthful. Perhaps it was kind after all.

"Thank you, black dragon." I stroked its body.

"Call me Zavilia. May I call you Fia?"

Bits of what had happened were coming back to me now. "Black dra—I mean, Zavilia. I think...I dreamed that we made a familiar pact last night."

"Heh heh, dream? It was nothing of the sort. The pact was made, sworn on my name. I am yours now. Examine your left wrist—you'll see the proof right there."

And there it was on my wrist, just as he said: a black ring, one millimeter thick, encircling my wrist.

"Distance is nothing to us now; this pact will allow me to come to you whenever you call, *wherever* you call. You may borrow some of my magic too, if you ask. As a matter of fact, you've *already* asked. I had to share magic with you yesterday, after your case of magic fatigue. You should be all right now, but how do you feel?"

"I...I dreamt I was a saint in my past life..."

"Heh heh, more dreams of reality? I can't speak for your past life, but you're certainly a saint in this one. My own actions had left me close to death. I regressed to infancy, but I couldn't heal fast enough. I'd made peace with my death when you saved me with your healing magic. Only an advanced spell could have saved me in that state...and only you could have cast it."

31

I shook my head. "But...I can't use magic."

"Memory is power. Your magic likely returned with your memories. We dragons do the same thing—we pass our memories down to our children, and we pass on our power with them."

Too much information, too fast. I needed time to think about everything, but...there was one thing I was absolutely certain of.

"Um, about me being a saint...could you keep that a secret? I...I was killed in my past life because I was a saint. I don't want that to happen again."

That's what the demon had promised, and it was the first thing that came to me when my memories returned. *I'll be killed if people know I'm a saint.*

Toyed with, tormented, humiliated, killed. And if I were ever reborn as a saint, he would find me and kill me the same way again.

Seeing me tremble, Zavilia reassured me: **"By your will, I will keep your secret. I'll always do what I can to protect you."**

Feeling abashed, I averted my gaze...and my eyes fell on the monster corpses encircling the two of us. "Uh... What's all...this?" I said, gesturing at the mess.

"The monsters were drawn in by the sweet scent of saint blood. These are their remains. They attacked all night, you know. Aren't *you* a popular girl?"

"But this many? There's at least fifty, maybe sixty? And they're all powerful too..." Mid-way through my sentence, I remembered what I'd come to this forest for. "The coming-of-age ceremony! Shoot, it's already morning! Oria's going to be worried sick about me!"

I took out a dagger and looked up at Zavilia. "Can I take the magic stones of these monsters?" He nodded, and I quickly cut open the closest monster for its magic stone. With that out of the way, I had to rush home. "Sorry, gotta go! My sister's waiting for me!"

"Wait. Get on." Zavilia slouched so I could climb on his back. Flying in on a black dragon would surely cause a ruckus, but I'd just have to deal with the fallout. I didn't want my sister gathering up all the knights in the domain and organizing a search party or something on my account...

Clinging tight to Zavilia, we took off for my estate.

A Tale of the
Secret
Saint

Leon, Second Son

MY NAME'S LEON RUUD, second son of the Ruud knight family. I inherited my father's brown hair and skill with the sword.

In a knight family, only those who become knights can be considered truly human. My father, my older brother, my older sister, and I...we were human. My younger sister Fia was subhuman.

And I was sure that she always would be, talentless as she was with the blade. She would never become a knight. She'd remain a waste of space that could die a dog's death for all I cared—that *should* die a dog's death, maybe.

Even so, Oria kicked up a fuss when Fia didn't return from the coming-of-age ceremony. Inexplicable, isn't it? If Fia couldn't clear something as simple as that ceremony, she would never become a knight. This was the simplest, cleanest way to be rid of her after her failure. The monsters and animals of the forest would clean up the corpse for us.

But Oria just *had* to form a search party. She even roped me into it. I couldn't object, since she was my senior in the brigade... even if it was just because she'd joined first.

Damn it, why do we have to meet for every stupid coming-of-age ceremony? I should've just skipped. I put my armor on, fastened my sword to my hip, and went out to join the search party gathering outside of the estate.

To my surprise, I found my older brother there as well. How in the world had Oria talked him into this?

I was overjoyed to see my brother and was on my way over to greet him when I heard a shout. "Hey, there's something in the sky!"

"It's a monster... It's...it's *huge*! And it's coming down fast!"

I turned and saw it—a monster darting towards us, its massive size evident even at this distance. A chill ran up my spine.

Oh no. That's a dragon, a black *dragon!* My mind went right to the Black Dragon King of legend, but...there was no way. If it was truly the legendary monster, we'd be doomed...

I drew my sword and called to my brother, "I'll do what I can to hold it off! Tell the brigade a monster has appeared!"

He didn't move, just stood there staring at the black dragon. Perhaps the fear had frozen him in place?

But then, my brother said the strangest thing.

"Isn't that Fia on its back?"

"Huh?!" Surely the fear was making him see mad delusions... Surely...? Dubious, I looked back at the dragon. My narrowed eyes went wide in astonishment.

The thing on the black dragon's back certainly did *look* like Fia. Perhaps the fear was making me see things as well.

Yes, that had to be it.

A Tale of the
Secret
Saint

6
The Results of the Coming-of-Age Ceremony

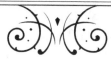

THERE WERE TWENTY-OR-SO PEOPLE gathered in front of the estate—a search party, I had to assume, with my sister standing right in the middle of it just like I'd predicted.

I had Zavilia descend to a spot about fifty meters in front of them, then slipped off his back and rushed to my sister. But before I could reach her, my oldest brother stepped in front of me.

Ardio Ruud was the first son of the Ruud family and a prodigy who had joined the knight brigade at only twelve years old—my own brother was the youngest person ever to earn his knighthood. His ice-cold beauty, aqua-teal colored hair, and mastery of the blade had earned him the nickname "The Knight of Ice."

"What's your relation to that black dragon?" His voice was flat and emotionless.

Was he talking to me? Was I...supposed to answer?

Ever since I could remember, Ardio had been a genius determined to make it big as a knight. He only made time for things that could make him stronger, and so for the last five years, I'd been dead to him.

And now that same Ardio was questioning me.

Shoot—I'm too nervous! I'm going to bite my tongue again like last time!

I spoke slowly and deliberately, "Zavilia and I...are friends."

All right! That answer was perfect!

No way could I admit I'd made a familiar pact with a legendary-class monster. If I did, I'd definitely slip up at some point and say, "Oh, it's because I'm actually a saint! Tee-hee!" or something like that. And they definitely wouldn't believe some passing dragon had decided to give me a ride out of the kindness of his heart. My answer was perfect! Aw yeah, go me!

While I was internally patting myself on the back, Zavilia turned his huge head away and sighed.

Ardio raised an eyebrow. "Only powerful monsters have names. And names serve as a direct link to their power, so they conceal them from all but those they pledge their service to."

"H-huh? Really? Um...oh, *ohhh*, you know what? Um, I met Zavilia's master and happened to hear them say his name. Yep!"

"If that was the case, you would have died thirty seconds ago. Monsters never allow those they don't approve of to speak their name."

Holy moly, really? That was an elite knight for you—knows everything about monsters and sharp as a tack. There was no way I could talk my way out of this, so...maybe I could just change the topic.

I thrust the magic stone I collected into my brother's hands. "Check out the stone I got for my coming-of-age ceremony!"

He looked at the magic stone, five centimeters in diameter, and narrowed his eyes.

Oh no. I remembered *that* face from when we were all kids. He only made it when he was about to scold or lecture me.

From behind him, my brother Leon hysterically exclaimed, "What the heck is that huge magic stone?! It's gotta be from at least an A-rank monster!"

Ardio looked at me with narrowed eyes and spoke with a deliberate, flat tone—he only acted like this when he was *furious*. "Most monsters are ranked on how difficult they are to slay, from lowly H-rank all the way to A-rank. But rarely, an S-rank is given, and an SS-rank is even rarer. That black dragon you brought along is an SS-rank. Even with a three-hundred-strong force of the strongest brigade captains and the most elite knights, I wouldn't be confident of victory against it."

"H-huh? I thought dragons were only as strong as a hundred normal knights."

"Normal dragons, yes. But a black dragon is an ancient and superior race, incomparable to such creatures."

"*Ohh.*"

"Furthermore, the size of a magic stone is proportional to the strength of the monster. Only A-rank monsters, requiring a squad of fifty knights to defeat, give this size magic stone...and you expect me to believe that you defeated one?"

"I-I'm sorry!" I exclaimed. Yeah, I had to come clean. No way an ordinary person like me could ever pull the wool over the eyes of a genius like him...

I bowed far enough to hide my face and admitted everything but the part about being a saint. "So, um, I found an injured black dragon in the forest that had reverted to an infant to heal. I *thought* it was a baby chick and used the healing potion I got from Oria to heal it and, as thanks, it made a familiar pact with me. But then I got tired, so I spent the night in the forest, and it turned out that Zavilia had killed the monsters that appeared overnight. That's how I got the magic stone. I'm sorry for lying!"

Leon looked bewildered. "You made...a familiar pact with the legendary black dragon...?" he muttered.

"Did you just call me a baby chick? Me, the Black Dragon King?" Zavilia muttered as well, even more bewildered.

"Your story is full of holes," said Ardio casually. "Healing potions are nowhere near as effective as an ancient dragon race's natural recovery—and yet the black dragon felt indebted enough to form a familiar pact with you?" He'd argued me into a corner like it was nothing.

Shoot—why does this genius have to be so pushy? Or is that just what geniuses are like? Cold sweat dripped down my back...

Then, my sister literally stepped in to save me, pushing past my brothers and making her way to the front. She slowly turned to face everyone present as she spoke. "Regardless of how, Fia has clearly made the black dragon her familiar. Any monster defeated by her familiar counts as a monster defeated by her. Everyone, this coming-of-age ceremony is over!"

"Huh?" Ardio began. "Sister, that's not the point of contention here—"

Oria cut him off and gave me a little push. "Look at you, Fia, you're a mess. Your hair's all disheveled, your face and clothes are covered in monster blood... Go wash up, okay? And everyone else, thank you for coming! Fia's back safely, so you may disperse!"

It was actually my own blood, but I wasn't about to correct her on that.

Realizing I forgot to thank Zavilia for flying me here, I turned back and met his eyes.

He bent down next to my ear and whispered, **"If anything happens, call for me. I'll be able to hear you from anywhere with the pact."**

The legendary, ancient Black Dragon King—the very same creature that took a bite out of my shoulder and flank, nearly sending me to the afterlife—was nose to nose with me. Though there was still part of me that was nervous about that, I didn't feel nearly as scared of him as I did before.

"Thank you, Zavilia. I'll see you later."

I didn't realize it then, but over the course of my past life and my current one, Zavilia was the first monster I ever befriended.

A Tale of the Secret Saint

Ruud Family Meeting

DOLPH—head of the Ruud family and vice-captain of the Fourteenth Knight Brigade—met the gaze of his eldest daughter. "Why have you called this family meeting, Oria?"

The Ruud family was gathered in the largest room in the estate—their father Dolph, the first son Ardio, the first daughter Oria, and the second son Leon. Fia was not present.

The topic of discussion? The girl who, moments prior, had ridden home on a black dragon.

"Father, what do you plan to do about Fia?" Oria asked, her expression betraying nothing.

Dolph stroked his chin in thought for a moment. "I suppose we should report her familiar to the knight brigade. Having a familiar is within one's rights and usually isn't reported, but a black dragon? A black dragon could spell trouble if left unchecked."

Oria nodded in agreement. "Wonderful decision, Father. You've already thought of the best way to raise the status of the Ruud name."

"What do you mean?" Dolph asked, confused by his daughter's vague compliment.

Oria's eyes went wide. "Father, you're aiming to become a captain, aren't you?"

"Of course I am! All knights aspire to either better serve their captain or to become one themselves!"

His daughter smiled sweetly as she lifted a hand into the air, pretending to give a toast with an imaginary chalice. "Then we must celebrate! To Father, who will soon be a captain thanks to the efforts of his daughter Fia!"

"What...is the meaning of this?" Dolph asked.

"Black dragons are the guardian beasts of Náv, and I've heard that the royal family desperately wants one within their direct influence. Once they hear that Fia has a pact with one, I'm sure they'll be clamoring to bring her into their ranks through marriage." Oria paused and smiled. "Aren't you lucky, Father. As soon as you report the black dragon, Fia will be married off and you'll be the father-in-law of a duke, or even a member of the royal family itself. You'll be made captain before you know it!"

"What?! I would never stoop to such dirty means to become captain!" Dolph bellowed.

Oria inclined her head. "Dirty means? Not at all. It's only natural to use your connections to rise through the ranks. You haven't made much progress as a vice-captain, have you? You're just as good as the other vice-captains, and there's nothing wrong with using your daughter to stand out from the pack."

"Absolutely not! I'd rather die than do something so disgraceful! One should become a captain through ability alone!"

Oria furrowed her brow, a troubled look crossing her face. "But...the moment you report Fia's black dragon, she'll be married off and you'll be promoted to captain. I'm sure all the other vice-captains will line up to congratulate you!"

"Never! I won't let them ridicule me for an unearned promotion... I will *never* report Fia's black dragon! And I'm sure...I'm *sure* this is some terrible misunderstanding! A black dragon is a legendary ancient beast—there's *no way* that Fia could make a pact with something like that! It must not be a black dragon at all, just some...blackish dragonish creature!" Roaring and scowling, he sent his chair toppling away as he stood up and made for the door.

"Y-you got that?!" he added, at the door. "Fia's familiar isn't a black dragon! Blackish! Dragonish! Creature!" He slammed the door, and his footsteps thundered as he marched away.

Oria gazed at the door with a satisfied grin before looking back at her brothers. "The head of the family has declared that Fia's familiar isn't a black dragon, and the head's words are absolute. I trust you two won't contradict this?"

"Wha—" Leon exclaimed. "Sister, you tricked him into saying that!"

Oria smirked. "Oh my, is my little brother of *lower rank* trying to offer his opinion? That's '*Elder* Sister' to you."

"Fine. *Elder* Sister, I'll respect your wish, but...truth be told, I don't think Fia's familiar is a black dragon either, let alone a

Black Dragon King. I mean, think about it! Fia is far too weak to be a knight. There's no way she got a legendary monster like the Black Dragon King to make a pact with her. You can't just luck your way into that! I won't spread any lies about Fia having something she clearly doesn't, no matter what she's deluded herself into thinking. A black dragon? No, it's just some...blackish dragonish monster!"

Oria nodded, satisfied, and then looked at her eldest brother.

Ardio sighed. "I'll obey Father's decision," he said indifferently. "Frankly, I'd rather not get involved at all. I'd rather just focus on myself as a knight." He glanced back at Oria and continued. "But you made one mistake in your little rant, intentional or not: the royalty and upper nobility would never marry Fia, even if that blackish dragonish familiar were a black dragon. They only marry saints."

Oria shrugged her shoulders. "I know that, of course. Personally, I think Fia's blackish dragonish familiar makes her far more valuable, but the royal family has some odd infatuation with the saints."

"Oria, hold your tongue!" Ardio warned.

"Yeah, yeah. Just thinking aloud," said Oria. She clearly knew just how disrespectful she was being.

"Anyway," she continued, "Fia's blackish dragonish familiar is a bit too small to be a black dragon. Perhaps it really is some other monster. I don't care much either way, as long as people aren't running around calling Fia 'The Black Dragon's Master' or something, tying her down." Oria stood up from her seat. "I'll go tell the other knights and squires of our domain about Father's decision," she said and swiftly left the room.

A week passed.

Even the ever-so-perfect Oria, daughter of the mighty Ruud family, can make a careless mistake now and then. She'd already returned to her knight brigade when she realized she'd forgotten to tell Fia herself not to speak of the matter.

Ah, shoot! Oria's brigade was far from the royal capital. *How could I have forgotten?! Oh, Fia, be careful...*

All she could do now was pray to the stars. Surely her prayers would reach Fia...wouldn't they?

A Tale of the
Secret
Saint

7
Testing New Powers

I SPENT THE NEXT THREE DAYS holed up in my room. There was just so much to think about and digest. I spent most of my time limp on my bed, zoning out.

On the fourth day, I got up to see my family off as they all returned to their brigades. Afterwards, I left my room and went behind the estate.

The days I spent in my room helped. Now I could clearly remember the three most important things that I'd learned when my past-life memories came rushing back to me.

First, about three hundred years had passed since my previous life as the Great Saint. Second, that life played out in the same country I was living in now. And third, although legends claimed that the current royal family was directly descended from the Great Saint, that was a lie—I'd never fallen in love, married, or had children before I died.

I sighed. Just thinking about my past life was making me depressed.

During my first lifetime, everyone could use magic. About ninety percent of people had healing magic, and the other ten percent had attack magic. But for some reason, healing magic consumed far more of a person's magical energy than attack magic did. Using healing magic even once would give a person magic fatigue. That was why saints made pacts with spirits, which let them use the mana in the air to cast healing magic at a nine-to-one ratio of mana to magic.

Now that I really think about it, spirit pacts were pretty incredible. Ten times the healing magic? No wonder everyone and their mother wanted to make one. For some reason, the spirits stopped making pacts with people, but I could only guess why.

In my past life memories, I knew that when a person made a pact with a spirit, proof of the pact would appear as a mark on the back of their hand. But I'd never heard anything about saints having that mark nowadays.

So where did the current saints get their power? My guess was that they were descendants of those who made pacts in the past. The spirits were kind; they allowed some of their gifts to be passed down to the pact maker's children and grandchildren. But those powers dwindled with each generation. Three hundred years ago, almost everybody chose to make a new pact, rather than rely on inherited power.

I didn't know exactly when the pacts stopped, but I guessed it was about a hundred years ago. That meant it had been three or four generations—the current saints were relying on pacts made by their grandmothers and great-grandmothers. Their healing powers couldn't be that strong. The ancestor's pact would have had to be with quite a powerful spirit for the effect to be at all noticeable after several generations.

There were probably a few people among the saints who had natural healing ability strong enough to use without a pact too, but abilities like that had always been incredibly rare.

That would explain why there were so few saints left...

And since there were so few magic healers left, those saints were revered.

Yup, I think I get it. I thought. *But, if...if somebody found out that I was a saint, then that demon would probably come looking for me and kill me. He promised he would...*

I was a healer, not a fighter. I hadn't been strong enough to cut the demon lord down myself. My three brothers from my past life were despicable people, but they were strong. Trying to do anything alone would just mean walking to my death.

So I made a decision.

I'll find three swordsmen who are at least as strong as my three brothers from my past life. Until I find them and team up with them, I won't use my saint powers! I looked up at the sky, feeling like I'd entered a new chapter of my life. *But, if at all possible, I still want to use this power for good.*

I shut my eyes and felt the magic coursing through my body. This was why I'd come behind the estate.

"Invigorate: Attack ×2; Speed ×2!" I cast strengthening magic and swung my blade horizontally, slicing cleanly through a ten-year-old tree.

"Wh-whoa!" I'd never done anything like that before...but I could make this work, right? I could use my past life's strength in secret—as long as I kept the power low and didn't overuse it, I'd be fine.

If I didn't use any healing magic, the demon wouldn't come looking for me. The current era called anybody who could use healing magic a saint, but the old meaning of the word only applied to people who made pacts with spirits. The demon would be looking for someone who'd made a pact.

As long as I didn't use any of the spirits' powers and left the mana in the air alone, I would be safe.

Safe... Is that why I wanted to be a knight so badly? Because somewhere deep down I remembered the threat the demon made, so I knew I had to be anything but a saint?

Well, there were three months until the knight brigade admission exam. Until then, I would try as many abilities as I could and figure out what I was capable of.

The Knight Brigade
Admission Exam

THREE MONTHS passed.

I was at the royal palace, waiting in line F for the admission exam. I'd arrived at the capital yesterday and had spent my time since then relaxing at the inn.

Wow...so many people. I looked at the bustle around me. They said that between five and ten thousand people applied every year, and it looked like they weren't kidding. It was hard to think that only a hundred of the people here were going to pass.

There were two separate admission exams held on different days. One was for knight school graduates only, and the other—the general exam block—was open to anyone. I was attending the latter today.

The knight school graduate exam block had about 150 applicants, and a hundred or so passed—much better odds than the general exam block. Normally, knight families like mine sent their children to knight school, but Ardio, the oldest, hadn't gone, so the rest of us siblings followed his example.

After experimenting with my Great Saint powers for the past three months, I found that I could use most of the same spells I'd known in my past life. I say "most" because some things like Magic Attack Protection or Cure Sickness required another person to test out. I wasn't sure whether those would work when put to the test, but I had to hope!

My magic reserves also matched what I remembered from my last life—about a thousand times larger than your average caster. Still, some powerful spells consumed a lot of magic and even I couldn't use them more than a few times.

The spirit pact I made in my previous life allowed me to use mana for ninety percent of a spell's cost, but that wasn't an option if I wanted to stay hidden. With just my own magic, I could only access one-tenth of my former power. I had to be careful how I used it.

I'd spent the first week of the three months figuring out what magic I actually had, and the remaining time I spent training. I'd never directly fought with anyone in my past life, so casting strengthening magic on myself while keeping my balance and using my sword techniques...it was all new to me. It was tough, but after three months I felt I was ready.

Today's the day I test my skills for real! Needless to say, I was excited.

The first stage of the exam was sparring with a knight. It was a simple test. All you had to do was block ten of the examiner's blows to pass.

Actually, Oria once told me she'd been an examiner at the

knight exam during her first two years of enlistment. I guess that meant that the examiners were chosen from the junior knights.

I looked towards the head of line F (we were divided up by the first letter of our names) and saw a familiar face.

"Weak! Can't be a knight if you don't brace yourself properly!" The examiner yelled as he sent an examinee's wooden sword flying.

Uh oh. I recognized that brown hair and those narrow eyes. It was—

"Annoying weaklings—I am the great Leon!"

Yes, *him*. It was Leon, my older brother, acting a bit reckless for an examiner. I watched as my brother sent wooden sword after wooden sword flying. Was the first stage of the exam really supposed to be this hard?

Sure, the point was to sift out the weak, but Leon had failed fifty people in a row...each on their first hit.

The other examiners exchanged blows and waited until the tenth exchange before knocking the wooden sword away—and about a fifth of their examinees passed. But my brother clearly didn't plan on passing anyone. He probably didn't even remember this was an exam anymore.

Maybe it was time for his sister to remind him.

But then I felt a tap on my shoulder. I turned around and found myself facing a broad, thoroughly ripped chest. Whoa... I could tell this person was buff even through the clothes. They were tall too; my eyes were chest-level when I turned.

I looked up to meet the eyes of a handsome, silver-haired man. He looked just like a prince from a fairy tale...

H-h-hot! So hot! I felt myself swoon, hard.

(Hey, don't judge me too harshly, okay? My previous life was pretty lacking in the romance department. How could I resist? And, I mean, I met his eyes at point-blank range—that's really intense and romantic, right?!)

But a moment later, I plummeted down from cloud nine. No man this handsome would talk to me unless he wanted to warn or scold me.

"I-I'm sorry," I stammered. "Are my clothes messy? Ah! Don't tell me, there's egg stuck in my teeth from breakfast!"

The silver-haired hottie—let's call him "Prince Charming" for now—furrowed his brows a bit. "I'm sorry if I surprised you. I couldn't help but notice our examiner is a little eccentric. He seems to be failing everyone, doesn't he? But the examiners have a responsibility to pass at least a fifth of us during the first stage, so I expect the other examiners will stop him. Soon he'll relent and start passing people. You might want to move to the back of the line to increase your chances. All the other women are lined up back there too, as you can see." He pointed to the back of the line and, sure enough, he was right.

Incredible! Such chivalry! And at the knight exam too! As a proper lady, I ought to show him my manners.

"Thank you kindly for your help." I bowed my head lightly, taking extra effort to appear grateful. I stepped out of the line and started walking towards the back, when...

"Hey, Fia! I see you!" Leon said, spotting me. "Don't you dare run away! Get over here!"

Ahh, Brother, why?! Prince Charming was so nice, and now... I cursed to myself. I met Charming's apologetic gaze and tried to wordlessly tell him that it was fine, I knew he meant well, and I didn't blame him for my getting spotted.

It must've been unusual for an examinee to be called by name. I felt all eyes on me (or at least the eyes of everyone in my line) as I ran up to my brother. "How dare you try to run away!" my brother bellowed. "You think you're special now, just because you got some blackish dragonish thing to be your familiar? C'mon, bring it!"

The examinees began to whisper among themselves...

"Did he just say, 'blackish dragonish thing'? Is that some kind of riddle?"

"He said 'familiar,' didn't he? Like, a monster?"

"No way, right? Monsters only make familiar pacts with humans stronger than themselves. We're not even knights yet..."

You're awful, Brother. I was trying my hardest not to stand out, and you blew it! I picked up a wooden sword and stepped onto the exam platform. I bowed once and swung, beginning the exam. I had to finish this before he ran his mouth any more.

In the smallest voice I could muster, I cast my strengthening magic. "Invigorate: Attack ×1.2; Speed ×1.2!"

My brother swung down on me, forcing me to take a step back as our wooden swords met. *Thwack!*

"Oh?" He looked surprised that I wasn't disarmed by the first blow.

He's strong! Despite strengthening myself, I was still forced to take a step back. He was leagues above me.

"*Invigorate: Attack ×1.5; Speed ×1.5!*" I recast my magic. Would it be enough, though? I gripped the hilt hard as we exchanged blows—*a second, third, fourth*. I maintained my poise, unlike in our first exchange. My brother gave me a perplexed look.

I sped up—*a fifth blow, a sixth, seventh, eighth, ninth*—I took a step forward as I placed my weight behind the last swing—*ten!*

With a *clunk*, my brother's sword flew away.

Shoot. I've done it now. I felt the eyes of all the examiners on me and stiffened. There was only one thing I could do now.

I smiled as sweetly as I could at my brother. "How considerate of you, sir! You went easy on me to meet your pass quota, didn't you? No wonder I barely managed to make it to the tenth exchange just then!"

My brother's mouth hung open.

C'mon, really? Make a face like that, and nobody's going to think he went easy on me. I need to get out of here. "If you will excuse me, then? Once again, thank you for going easy on me." Forcing my brightest smile, I quickly made for the door.

Laughter erupted from where silver-haired Prince Charming had been, but I wasn't about to turn around and see it. No, I ran away as fast as my legs could take me.

This year there were about seven thousand total applicants, and about fourteen hundred (in other words, twenty percent) made it to the second stage...the written exam. We were split into groups of a hundred each and led to different rooms. I took a seat at a desk.

"You have an hour and forty minutes for the exam. Begin!" As soon as the examiner declared the start of the exam, hands went up.

"I forgot a writing utensil!"

"Me too!"

"Ditto!"

Yeah, seems about one-third of the examinees forgot something to write with. The examiner quickly passed out writing utensils to the ones who raised their hands.

Still feeling a bit unsettled over what just happened, I looked down at the first question on the sheet.

QUESTION ONE:

Draw the knight brigade uniform.

I stared in blank amazement at the question before looking up at the examiner...who was wearing said uniform. Everyone in the room began to draw it.

Is this a joke question? One of those free spaces on a bingo card? Why else would they put this question on the exam if they knew a uniformed officer would be proctoring? My brain raced, trying to find a logical answer.

"Ha ha, c'mon, guys. You should be focusing on your exam, not looking at me." The examiner chided us with a grin on his face.

It...isn't a joke?

QUESTION TWO:

You see a boy being chased by a boar and a girl running after an apple that's rolling away from her. What do you do?

H-huh? What's that supposed to mean? I guess I'll skip it for now...

QUESTION THREE:

A senior knight is badmouthing the captain. What do you do?

Wh-what? Isn't the written exam supposed to be easy? I have to write something, though. Um...how about this?

"I would agree with the senior knight. He'd said 'The captain's too strong! He's practically a monster!'"

There we go! That was really a compliment, so there's nothing to be mad about! Easy-peasy! Back to question two...

"I would kick the boar with my right foot while catching the apple with my left hand."

Perfect! I got this!

Overflowing with baseless confidence, I steamrolled my way through the rest of the questions.

In the end, it seemed almost impossible to fail the second stage, meaning the real dealbreaker was the third stage: the sword skill practical. Both the first and third stages were basically tests of sword skill. All that really mattered for knighthood was prowess with the sword.

Figures.

Around one hundred examiners stood atop a raised platform. They seemed to be decently seasoned knights, in their mid-twenties to mid-thirties.

The examiner in the middle explained the practical in a booming voice. "The third stage of the exam will be a three-minute mock battle with an examiner. Two other examiners will judge your performance. Lose the battle or win, you *will* pass if your skills are found sufficient. You may use a sword you've brought with you or we will provide you with one. The examiners will use metal swords with their edges dulled. That is all."

I decided to use my own sword, which I'd received from my father after my coming-of-age ceremony. It looked like any other sword, but I'd actually loaded it up with magic enhancements—Attack ×2 and Speed ×2, to name a few. These enhancements would normally give the sword a glow, but I'd applied Veil, a camouflage spell, to the weapon.

Heh heh...applying magic to weapons was actually a long-lost technique, so this sword was incredibly valuable. The only way for most people to get an enhanced weapon was to buy an expensive "Legacy of the Golden Age," a magic weapon named after the era it was made in. The other option was to search labyrinths for treasure chests.

Concealing the sword's glow hid its true value. I wouldn't want this to get stolen, you know?

Looking around, I saw most examinees decided to use their own sword, likely because they were accustomed to it. Most of their swords looked like mine too—that is, cheap. It was the general exam block, after all. Those from noble or knight families were likely in the knight school graduate exam block, which meant most of the examinees today were either the children of merchant families or adventurers a few years into their careers.

The third stage of the exam was also divided alphabetically, so I stood in line F once again. I made sure to line up at the end this time and found myself grouped with most of the women.

The testing was already underway. A quick glance was all I needed to see how strong the examiners were; these battles were like watching an adult humor a child. I guess I shouldn't have been surprised. Knights fight enemy soldiers and monsters on a day-to-day basis, after all.

The examiner called up the next person, the silver-haired Mr. Handsome from earlier.

Oh, thank goodness, I thought. *He made it too!*

I watched in awe as he fought the examiner. He was miles ahead of the other examinees in terms of strength, on par with the experienced knight he was fighting.

Amazing! Could he actually win? But then I noticed a change. His strikes slowed and weakened, and he was gradually pushed back.

Without thinking, I moved closer to get a better look. He was hurt... His right arm was definitely broken.

The examiner didn't seem to notice, but he wasn't a Great Saint. As for me, I could discern injuries at a glance. The pain must've been unbearable. Sweat dripped down his face as his swings continued to slow, but he still didn't let the pain show on his face.

Clang! His sword went flying from his hands, landing right beside me.

"Sorry!" he said, approaching me. "Are you all right?" Up close, I could see his face was flushed and his breathing ragged; sweat clung to his hair and clothes.

Whoa. Even with a broken arm, he trudged through the pain and fought without a word of complaint. How much self-control did this guy have?

I picked up his sword and passed it to him, brushing against his right arm as I did so. "Grant this arm the benediction of protection," I whispered, omitting the core phrase normally used. This would make the spell weaker than normal, but it would at least take the pain away for the next five minutes.

"Hm?" He looked at his arm in surprise.

"You should go," I said, bringing him back to his senses. "The examiner is waiting."

"Ah, r-right!"

He resumed the mock battle, his movements faster and stronger than before. He held his ground against the examiner.

As for the examiners judging him...

"Whoa..."

"Holy..."

...they made no effort to hide their surprise.

An hour passed, and then another. Finally, my turn came. I really regretted joining the back of the line now.

There were only two more people ahead of me when an examiner from another line called out to ours. "We've finished with our line. Please send some of yours our way."

Aw, nuts. I could recognize that silky tenor anywhere... Ardio, my oldest brother. I fell to my knees the moment I saw his face. *Why, Brother?!* I wanted to scream. All the other examiners had simply left once they finished with their lines.

I shot a death glare at Ardio, hoping he'd pick up on my feelings. *Please, just leave!* But he didn't notice, and I was moved to his line with a few others.

What are the odds I'd face both of my brothers at the knight exam? Actually, won't people suspect they went easy on me if I pass?

Ardio coolly stepped onto the platform as I quietly fumed.

The other two examinees looked moved.

"No way! The Knight of Ice is going to fight us himself? That's incredible!"

"It's an honor, sir!"

No, no, no, this ain't an honor at all! My brother doesn't know the meaning of the word "restraint"! He's going to beat us black and blue!

Sure enough, the two examinees conceded quickly. The first lasted two minutes. The second, just one. Go figure.

It had been a while since I last saw Ardio fight, but his fighting style was still perfectly by the book—precise and flawless. The gap between us was too wide; I had no chance of winning against him in an honest fight—not without a special technique, anyway.

"Fia, don't hold back. Attack me as if you intend to kill," my brother said.

Heh, nice try. That won't work on me! I bet you just want me to lose my cool so you can get an easy counter in. Irked, I decided to cheat a little. I reached into my breast pocket, took out the magic stone from the monster Zavilia killed, and placed it into a hole in the pommel of my sword.

Equipment can only be enhanced to a certain point, depending on the material it's made of. My sword, for instance, had "Attack ×2" and "Speed ×2" as its limit. Magic stones, on the other hand, could be enhanced with magic far further. This valuable magic stone with a diameter of five centimeters, only obtainable from an A-rank monster, was enhanced with a powerful, *powerful* magic enhancement.

I stepped onto the platform and faced my brother. "Ardio, how about I give you a taste of my special technique? It's called... Lightning Swing!" I said proudly.

"*Hmph.* You should reconsider that name," he said flatly, narrowing his eyes. "You sound like an uneducated child."

Again with the lecturing! It was my *special technique; I should be allowed to name it what I want!*

As soon as we were given the signal to start, I dashed forward and swung.

Clack...

...thwomp.

Our swords only needed to meet once for his knees to give out from under him.

"Aha ha ha ha ha ha! Now you know the power of the... Lightning Swing!" I really belted the name out to rub it in.

My brother had a knee on the ground and used his sword to support his upper body. He struggled to look up and glare at me. "What is this?"

"A status ailment. This sword has a one hundred percent chance to apply paralysis."

"What?!" He looked up at me in disbelief. "Where did you get that magic sword? From your blackish dragonish familiar?! And...the paralysis, when does it wear off?!"

"I don't know. Thirty minutes? An hour? At the very least, it'll take longer than three minutes. But the judges don't know what's going on. As long as I just stand here holding my sword out like this, I'll automatically pass when time's up!"

"You...you would take such a cheap victory?"

"A win's a win. As the loser, you have no right to speak against me."

"I don't recall teaching you such crooked chivalry."

"Ha ha, of course you don't. You've ignored me for the last five years, after all. And what did you *ever* teach me?"

My brother glared at me. "I'll remember this, Fia!"

Oh nooo, so scary. Ha, was that cheap line the best you could do?

My brother stayed on his knee glaring up at me until our three minutes were up. To everyone present, including the judges, I had defeated "the Knight of Ice" in just one blow.

Only when I returned to the inn did I realize...I'd stood out just as much in the third stage as I had in the first.

A Tale of the
Secret
Saint

9
Admission Exam Results

THE KNIGHT BRIGADE admission exam results were announced ten days later.

I nervously ran my eyes up and down the notice board looking for my exam number and breathed a sigh of relief when I found it. I passed.

The day after the exam, I'd remembered (all too late) that the third stage was judged by how well you fought, not whether you won or not. Would the judges think my fighting style was too underhanded and unchivalrous? In my past life, it never mattered *how* I won, just that I survived. But in this one, I had to keep appearances in mind. I'd have to think things through a bit more from here on out.

It was supposed to be a test of sword skill, but I cheated with an enchanted magic stone. It feels kind of...cheap.

"Ha ha ha..." An empty, despondent laugh spilled out of my mouth. I shuffled over to a chart that listed where all the new recruits were assigned. Annoyingly, many of the other knights-to-be were on the taller side, and they completely obstructed my view of the board. I was standing to the side, waiting for the crowd to thin out, when I heard a voice.

"Hello."

I turned around to find silver-haired Mr. Handsome I'd met in line F back during the exam.

He smiled sweetly, holding out his right hand for a hand-shake. "I take it you passed as well then, seeing as you're looking for your brigade assignment?"

Whoa, he was utterly dazzling! Absolutely fairy-tale prince material...

"May I introduce myself? My name is Fabian, eldest son of the Marquess Wyner, seventeen years old. It's a pleasure to make your acquaintance."

"Oh? Um?" I couldn't hide my surprise. *Marquess? As in, upper nobility? As in, there are only nine or ten in the whole country? And he's the* eldest *son?! That's like...the heir!*

"Um..." I swallowed. "I thought marquesses were just an urban legend. They're real?!" Listen, I may have been a princess in my previous life, but I spent most of my time cooped up in the castle or out killing monsters. I rarely met with nobles then, and I'd *never* met a noble in this life. How could I, with my social status?

Fabian didn't seem to mind my outburst. "To be more precise, my father is the marquess, not me. But I assure you, they are real."

"Oh, er, um...? I'm Fia, second daughter of the Ruud knight family, fifteen years old. It's a pleasure to meet you."

"Fia... I thought so. I noticed 'Fia' was the only female name on the passing list that started with 'F,' so I figured that had to be you. Is it all right if I call you by your first name? You may call me 'Fab,' if you'd like."

"Huh? Oh, uh..."

"I've been looking for you, Fia. I'm in your debt, you see. When I gripped my sword after you picked it up during the third stage of the exam, I felt the pain in my arm go away." Fabian took my right hand in both of his and gave me a heartfelt look.

"Uh..." I froze up. *Is that it? Does he know about my healing magic? No...no way. Nobody would expect to just run into a saint, especially not at a knight's exam. He must think it's just a coincidence...right?*

I looked down at the hands gripping my own and was surprised to see that his broken arm was healed. *You're kidding... His bone healed in just ten days?*

"Um... You said your arm was hurt?" I asked. "Is it better now?"

"It is. It was painful, but I took some healing potion and had a saint finish healing it. It wouldn't do for a new recruit to join with a broken arm, after all."

I'd heard it was difficult for anyone but knights to see a saint, but I guessed the influence of a marquess family could do it. But how'd he get hurt in the first place?

He smiled wryly, perhaps reading my expression. "The family cat got stuck in a tree after jumping from the veranda of the fourth floor. I climbed the tree, grabbed the cat, and fell right off. That's how I broke my arm."

"Oh." My image of a perfect, dazzling prince was rapidly disintegrating.

"It was the morning of the knight school graduate exam block too. Naturally, I had to give up on taking the exam that day and instead applied for the general exam block. I cursed my luck then, but I *did* get to meet you, eh? Perhaps it was destiny..."

"Oh. Um..." Yikes. It looked like he was a womanizer—I'd heard that a lot of nobles were like that.

I started to back away when he grabbed my arm and dropped a bomb of a smile on me. "And guess what, Fia? We've both been assigned to the First Knight Brigade."

"We...what?"

The First Knight Brigade? No way! Of the twenty brigades, the First Knight Brigade was the best of them all. There's no way they'd assign fresh recruits there...right?

"It usually takes ten years of experience to get assigned to the First Knight Brigade and guard the royal family; the same is true of the Second Knight Brigade, which guards the Royal Castle. It seems that the two of us are breaking records," he explained, smiling broadly. I had frozen stiff as a board again, this time in disbelief.

He continued, "The Third Mage Knight Brigade and the Fourth Monster Tamer Knight Brigade have some special exceptions, but most new recruits are either sent to the Fifth Knight Brigade to guard the royal capital, to the Sixth through Tenth Knight Brigades to exterminate monsters, or to the Eleventh through Twentieth Knight Brigades—the border patrol."

I couldn't even muster up a reply. My mind spun with the same thought over and over. *If I'm assigned to guarding the royal family, I have to meet the descendants of my past life's brothers, the same ones who left me for dead. And I had to protect them? Ugh... can I even manage it? Perhaps I should be the one to leave them for dead this time...*

"Uh, Fia, are you okay?"

"Oh, sorry. I was just lost in thought. Um...who's the current royal family?" I blurted.

"The royal family currently only consists of two people, His Majesty the King and his younger brother. His Majesty himself has announced this, so I can speak freely on the matter: it seems he is incapable of loving a woman and has declared his younger brother next in line for the throne."

"Wh-whuh?!" My eyes went wide, completely blindsided.

"The younger brother in question is, as you surely already know, the leader of all twenty brigades—the captain himself."

"What?!"

"I...take it you didn't know, then."

Of course I know the captain. He's a legend. They say he fought all the captains of the brigades simultaneously and won. I can't even count on my fingers how many times I've heard tales of his feats, and now you're telling me he's royalty on top of all that?

"I've been living in the countryside for all my life," I whispered, embarrassed, "so I'm a little out of the loop..."

Fabian thought for a bit, before continuing, "You'll see him tomorrow at the welcome ceremony. The rumors don't even

A TALE OF THE SECRET SAINT

cover... You'll understand when you see him. Now, shall we go collect our uniforms? The lapel pin is different for each brigade, so be sure to get the right one. We should get to sleep early too, in preparation for tomorrow."

He practically dragged me to where they distributed uniforms. I'd already told them I was assigned to the First Knight Brigade and received my uniform when I realized I still hadn't seen the brigade assignment chart for myself.

Oh no. Was I really in the First Knight Brigade? Fabian seemed kinda airheaded now that I knew him, and maybe he'd made a mistake. Oh gosh. What if I showed up and they chased me out on the first day?!

The Welcome Ceremony

THE DAY OF THE WELCOME CEREMONY was met with clear skies.

I put on the uniform I received yesterday and looked at myself in the mirror. The knight uniforms used blue as a base color to represent a knight's ideals and loyalty, with black for contrast. On the collar was proof that I was a member of the First Knight Brigade, a lapel pin with a black dragon—the royal family's coat of arms.

"Not bad. I'm looking, what, twenty percent better than usual?" Feeling cooler than I'd ever felt before, I struck a pose... and that's when I caught sight of a woman in the reflection gazing at me with deadpan eyes over my shoulder. "Ah! Ms. Olga! I'm sorry you had to see that, and first thing in the morning too!"

Olga simply handed me a cup of something hot and waved her hand as if to tell me not to worry. "I thought I told you to just call me 'Olga'. Next time you add the 'Ms.' I'm ignoring you."

"...Understood, Olga."

"No need to be so stiff either. We're colleagues. Save it for your squad leader or captain; that's what everyone else does."

"Unders... Got ithb." Shoot—bit my tongue again.

She laughed heartily at that. "Oh, you're a riot! How many times does that make since yesterday?"

Olga was my new roommate. The day the exam results were announced, all knights soon to be working in the royal capital—in other words, the First through Sixth Brigades—were allowed to move into the knight dormitories. The dorms were split by gender and brigade. For all but the highest ranked, it was two to a room with a shared bathroom and bathtub.

As for Olga herself, she was a tall woman with blonde hair and pale skin. She was twenty-seven years old and in her twelfth year in the knight brigade, her second year with the First Knight Brigade specifically. She was laid-back enough to treat me as an equal despite me being more than ten years her junior.

"You better get going," she said. "New recruits gotta arrive early."

"*Eep!* Yeah, that's right! I should leave right now just in case I get lost." I bolted out of the room and out of the women's dorm, only to find Fabian waiting at the entrance.

Noticing me, he waved with a smile. As for me, *ohhhhh*, he was so hot, I was about to melt into a puddle on the spot. He was beyond dashing in his knight uniform, the very image of a perfect, dazzling prince.

"Good morning, Fia. It didn't feel right going to the ceremony alone, so I waited for you. I hope that's all right."

"S-sorry that I got full of myself and thought I looked twenty percent better in uniform..."

"Twenty...what?"

(Agh, I had the sudden urge to hide in a hole and never come out. And I'd been so stupidly proud staring at myself in the mirror...!)

"Fia?"

"That's me! And it's nothing! I just got kinda full of myself thinking I looked good in uniform, but you brought me to my senses, you know?"

"I...really don't," he said with a sweet, rather confused smile. "But I'm glad I could help?"

It was only morning and I already wanted to curl up in bed. I continued to mentally berate myself for my blind vanity as I followed Fabian to the welcome ceremony.

The ceremony was held on the knight training grounds within the castle walls. Around two hundred new knight recruits were in attendance alongside all the captains and vice-captains, as well as all the members of the First through Sixth Knight Brigades already stationed within the royal capital.

The ceremony program went like this: first, the captain would address everyone, then a representative for this year's knight recruits would make a speech, and finally, one of the incoming knight recruits and one of the existing knights would have an exhibition match.

The scary thing was that the chosen representatives would be announced on the spot. Being the big chicken I was...what if I got unlucky and had to give a speech?

I stood in file at the center of the field with all the other new recruits. Gradually, the other knights gathered grouped by brigade, forming a half-circle that boxed us in. By my estimate, there were around two hundred knights present from each of the attending six brigades—a total of around twelve hundred knights.

Even from a distance, these knights were clearly elite. Each and every one of them stood perfectly at attention, their well-trained bodies clad in either uniforms or armor with a sword at every hip.

Just when I thought everyone had gathered, a small group of around fifty knights entered, all wearing white uniforms—white being the color that symbolized faith and integrity. Those uniforms were only allowed to be worn by vice-captains or above. This group all carried themselves differently from the rest. Their appearance suddenly shifted the mood, the indistinct chatter giving way to a tension that spread across the crowd.

The tension peaked, and a single knight entered. Despite how crowded it was, I could clearly make out the sound of his boots as he walked. You could hear a pin drop in the sudden silence.

The knight exuded an aura unlike any other, commanding attention with his presence alone. But even more unusual was the absolute respect and deference the surrounding knights regarded him with. One by one, they bowed. Even the captains lowered their heads as he passed, as if his form were too great to take in directly. Before I knew it, the only one without their head lowered was him—captain of the Náv Black Dragon Knights, Saviz Náv.

Saviz stepped onto the platform and addressed everyone in a clear, resounding voice. "Let us rejoice at the arrival of our new comrades."

No one said a word, for fear they might miss his voice. It was like his voice itself was gospel, like he himself was a god.

He was taller than any other knight present. He wore the white uniform of the high-ranking knights, with black and gold colors as contrast. A black mantle with red lining was draped over one shoulder. His hair was the same black luster as his mantle, reaching down to the nape of his neck. Just beneath his bangs were eyes of dark obsidian, an elegantly straight nose, and a pair of thin lips. All came together...perfectly. But the aspect of his face that stood out the most was the black eyepatch covering his right eye. That small asymmetry took away none of his appeal—if anything, it made all his other features stand out more.

"As knights," he said, his voice echoing in our hearts, "we pledge to strive towards self-betterment. We pledge to never take from, deny, nor abandon those who we serve. We pledge to uphold the Ten Knight Commandments and serve our kingdom and its people until our last breath. Glory to the Náv Black Dragon Knights!"

The knights saluted with their right hands over their hearts and echoed his words in chorus. "Glory to the Náv Black Dragon Knights!"

The whole spectacle was breathtaking.

I stared at Saviz in admiration, and I could tell the others around me were doing the same thing. As a princess in my past life, I'd heard royal speeches quite a few times—from my father, from my brothers, or from a neighboring country's king—but I'd never heard a speech as enthralling as his.

There was just something about him that drew you in. Whether it was some innate personality trait or a skill he'd learned was lost on me, but he was clearly no common man.

I continued to stare in admiration at Saviz when he suddenly... met my gaze?

Hm? Did he just...? No, it couldn't be. It's probably that thing really good lecturers do where it feels like they look everybody in the eye. There's no way he'd notice me, right?

Next, a representative of the incoming knight recruits was going to say some words—no doubt it would be a nerve-racking task after the captain's moving speech. The unlucky recruit chosen as representative was none other than Fabian.

Yeah, no surprise. He was a fresh recruit assigned to the First Knight Brigade right off the bat, an unprecedented occurrence. Which means...it just as easily could've been me?! Whew, thank goodness he's here...

I watched Fabian as he bowed politely to the senior knights and gave a short speech about duty and hard work. He looked nervous as he spoke but managed to do it all without slipping up, likely due to his aristocratic upbringing.

Now all that was left was the exhibition match.

I heard some clamor from the knights presiding over the ceremony. I thought it was strange, but Fabian had just returned, so I turned my attention to him.

"Hey, good job!" I said. "You did it all without biting your tongue once!"

"I...don't think most people worry so much about biting their tongue, but...thank you."

The announcer started speaking again, but this time his voice seemed strained. "We will now begin the exhibition match. The chosen representative of the new recruits is...Fia Ruud of the First Knight Brigade."

"Blrggh?" I looked back at the announcer, mouth agape, feeling dopey.

He coughed a few times before squeaking out, "Um, and her opponent will be...*ahem*...Saviz Náv, captain of the Náv Black Dragon Knights!"

Huh?

This time, I didn't say a thing. I didn't have the breath to do it.

The knights were in an uproar, particularly the captains.

"What?! Y-you want the captain himself to participate?! Is this a joke?!"

"N-no, the captain himself ordered this..."

"Huh?! Then I should be his opponent! I'll fight the captain!"

"I-I cannot! The exhibition match is meant to be a symbol of learning from your seniors. It must be between an experienced knight and a new recruit!"

"Fine! Hurry up and bring out this Fia Ruud! Who are they?!

And why the hell was some new recruit put in the First Knight Brigade, anyway?!"

Oh no! Wh-what do I do?! I was in a real pickle, and none of it was my fault.

Fabian looked at me sympathetically. "Um...try your best, I guess? The captain is known for things like killing A-class monsters single-handedly or defeating a thousand soldiers by himself, so...nobody will think badly about how you do, okay?"

There he was, trying to preemptively soften the blow of my upcoming loss. I appreciated the sentiment, but it wasn't exactly what I needed right now.

"Y-yeah," I stammered. "Normally the exhibition match would be with a knight five years your senior. You typically wouldn't see a squad leader participate, much less the c-c-captain..."

Even though I'd never spoken to any of them before, my fellow recruits cheered me on with some surprising words of support. "Just one strike, Fia! Just block one strike and you'll be a hero!"

I walked forward, trying to look as small as possible. The crowd looked taken aback as they saw me...

"Huh? They picked some kid?"

"Ain't she a tad tiny? She won't even serve as an appetizer for the captain! Why'd they choose *her*?"

"Poor thing, she's going to get massacred. Oh, I can't watch..."

Complaints and concerns all around—just imagine how I felt. At that point I had tears in my eyes, and I was so nervous that I could hardly move. It took everything I had just to shuffle one foot in front of the other.

Desperate for help, I looked back at the new recruits I'd just left and was surprised to find...nobody. They'd joined the surrounding brigades to get a better view of the exhibition match.

You're all awful! I couldn't help thinking to myself. *I'm not your entertainment, you know!*

I stood there, knees wobbling, when my brothers ran up to me. "Y-you guys!" I was moved to tears—or *more* tears, anyway. *I guess blood really is thicker than water...*

"Listen up, Fia!" said Leon. "You've used up a lifetime's worth of luck getting to this moment, so you gotta do everything you can to fight even just a second longer! Even if it kills you, got it?!"

How...nonsensical.

"Listen carefully, Fia," said Ardio. "Knights never give up, even in the face of overwhelming odds. So...who knows? Perhaps an ant may fell a dragon. That possibility only exists as long as you don't give up, do you understand?"

How...overdramatic and useless.

The two of them looked dead serious as they said the most inane things I could imagine. But then again, my brothers *were* knight-nuts—absolutely fanatic about knighthood and nothing else. *And aren't I the same?* I thought. *I've waited so long to become a knight, and here I am. What is there to fear now?*

But even though their words were idiotic, they did calm me down. I turned around and began to pace towards Saviz, only to find he had already approached me.

"Your name is Fia, I believe?" he said, his mantle already discarded.

"Aieee!" Leon shrieked. "The captain just said *my* sister's name!" Ardio quickly carted him away to keep him from causing trouble.

Even some distance away, I could feel an overwhelming pressure emanating from him. Maybe it was the size of his muscles or maybe the sheer intensity of his presence itself...but whatever it was, I could feel goosebumps forming on my skin.

He seemed unfazed by the twelve hundred pairs of eyes watching him. Facing me, twenty meters or so away, he drew his sword.

"I won't strike," he said. "You can give it your all."

What a man! I thought. *A military hero and royalty to boot, but he's still giving a new recruit like me a proper chance? No way am I going to waste his kindness and give him a half-baked fight. That would be disrespectful! And if I'm disrespectful... Oh no, what if the other knights kill me?!*

I put my hand on my sword sheath and whispered, "Invigorate: Attack ×3, Speed ×3." My sword's enhancements probably wouldn't be enough, so I enhanced my body as much as I could. But still, one glance at him filled me with despair.

How? Why? What is he?!

Saviz looks like a monster...or did he transform into a monster somehow? I bet that's it. Even Zavilia can't compare to this guy.

As a saint, I couldn't just sense injuries—I could also determine someone's strength just by looking at them. That skill was important for conserving magic. Knowing how strong an enemy was meant that I knew how much power I needed to block their attack.

Heh...but even with all my gimmicks, the only advantage I have is that I might be faster...

Stronger than Zavilia...I could practically see the black dragon looming behind Saviz.

"My name is Fia Ruud!" I raised my voice and performed the knight salute. "It is an honor to receive your guidance!"

Biting my lip, I steeled myself and walked forward. When I was about five meters away, I dashed forward and drew.

Our swords met with a clear, resounding *clang*. He squinted just slightly, studying me, strength surging through his body as he blocked. My sword strike wasn't weak—I could feel the harsh impact of my blow as our swords met—but it was nowhere near enough.

He was strong. I hadn't used the paralysis-inducing magic stone out of respect for the captain, but I bet he could've just shrugged it off with sheer willpower.

I retreated for a moment, stepped back in, and swung at his left side three times. Feinted, swung at his right. Left again. Our swords met with each strike, metal shrieking. The crowd began to murmur around us—there was something peculiar about the sound of our blades.

"H-how is she so fast?"

"More importantly, what is that sword?! Can you hear that?"

I retreated again and leapt to Saviz's right.

"Haah!"

Left, left, left, left, and another strike, left!

"Tsk!" He clicked his tongue and, for the first time in the entire battle...pushed back against my sword.

It went flying.

"W-we have a winner! Captain Saviz!" the judge cried. The cheering fell silent. Now the knights simply stared.

Saviz shot me a vicious glare. I met it with an awkward smile as I looked back at him from the ground—I'd fallen right on my butt after that last exchange.

U-um... Did I do something wrong?

"My win is invalid! I swore I wouldn't strike, but in the end, I did!" Saviz declared. The few knights who had begun to cheer immediately went silent as the grave. "Fia Ruud."

"Y-yes?!"

"Show me your sword. That speed and power you demonstrated earlier is far beyond your natural ability."

Eeek! My, what keen eyes he has...

I rushed to pick up my sword and held it out to him, trembling all the while.

He looked blankly at my plain, unadorned sword before taking it with his right hand and lightly swinging it. The air ripped unnaturally as he swung, stirring up a dust cloud.

"The speed and attack power of this sword has been enhanced. Multiple times, in fact—I've never seen such a thing. There's even camouflage magic... Yes, it appears to be a Veil to hide its glow." Without so much as turning around, Saviz summoned someone. "Cyril!"

A knight rushed out from among the captains and vice-captains. He wore the white uniform of a captain with a sash, the color of which marked him as captain of the First Knight Brigade.

Oh, so that's my direct superior!

He had blue eyes, and his hair was light gray. He must've been in his late twenties, and he was well built just like the captain. There wasn't that overwhelming sense of *presence,* though. His build was more on the slender side, and he gave off an air of refinement.

"Cyril, hold out your sword," Saviz demanded. "I'd like to test this."

Cyril obeyed with a faint smile. I couldn't help but eye his sword as he drew it. It was a beautiful silver color—the color of mithril. Mithril swords cost practically a hundred times more than your standard sword. Being captain must pay really well.

He held up his mithril sword and pointed it at the sky. Moments later, Saviz took a light step forward, another step at a blinding speed, and he swung. The two blades made contact— and with a loud clang, Cyril's sword snapped in half.

"This cannot..." Cyril trailed off, staring at the remainder of his sword in disbelief. "Sir, my sword was made of mithril. No ordinary iron sword could break such a weapon. How was your swing so powerful?! And that lightning-quick step, what was that?!"

"I suspect your subordinate has your answer. Am I right, Fia?"

Ohhh craaaaaap. I wanna curl up into a ball.

Attack power can actually be quantified. For instance, the average knight has an attack of about 100. Enhancements normally take the form of flat bonuses like +10 or +15, because that's what normal enchanters know how to do.

That's where I screwed up. I'd used the Great Saint's unique method of enhancing, learned from the spirits, and gave my sword a ×2 enhancement. With my lowly attack of 80, that was nothing. But for Saviz? No wonder he'd shattered that sword.

Ugh! Stupid, stupid, Fia! Why didn't I just put a +80 enhancement on it?

"Fia, this sword is on par with the national treasures," said Saviz. I didn't dare look up, though. I just stayed knelt where I was. What was I even supposed to say?

"This sword's enhancement," he continued, "easily surpasses Attack +100 or even Attack +200. The same goes for its speed."

Yes and no, sir! These enchantments don't add. They multiply! Not that I could just tell him that.

"The power I feel in this sword...it's surely akin to the might of a demon."

A demon?! I wanted to exclaim.

Okay. Okay, I could still turn this thing around. "The truth is, that sword..."

The knights around us listened with bated breath.

I took a deep breath. "The truth is...that sword was given to me by my father as a gift for my coming-of-age ceremony!"

A surprised yelp rang out from the brigade captains and vice captains. It was the vice-captain of the Fourteenth Knight Brigade, Dolph Ruud...my father.

"Wh-what are you talking about?! I just picked a random sword from the family armory; there's no way it's as powerful as a national treasure!" He turned away from me and began profusely apologizing to Saviz. "If I'd known it was such a powerful sword, I would've given it to the kingdom! Forgive me!"

That sounded about right. He *had* given me a perfectly ordinary, perfectly regular sword.

He continued to apologize to Saviz, swearing he would give him the sword and have his underlings check the rest of the weapons in his armory. And *finally* the spotlight was off me! I took the opportunity to try to fade back into the group of recruits when Saviz stopped me.

"Wait."

"Yeshpf!" Oww.

Gentleman that he was, Saviz was kind enough to not comment on me biting my tongue. "One last question: during the exhibition match, why did you focus on attacking my left side?"

Oh! I can actually answer that one! I put on my serious face and said, "It's because I have my chivalry as a knight, sir. I would never take advantage of your blind side, especially not when you were so gracious as to promise not to strike back."

Nailed it! I thought, with a mental fist-pump.

As enthusiastic as I was, Saviz looked dissatisfied. "Is that so?

Does your *chivalry* permit stooping low enough to use a magic sword in a fair fight?"

Um, yes and no?! The enhancements are actually applied by me, so the sword's strength is technically my strength, if you think about it, kinda? Not that I could actually say any of that. *Oh man, I was so sure that answer was good enough.*

I glanced up to find his sharp gaze fixated on me. Unable to bear it any longer, I answered truthfully. "It does. I figured it would dishonor you if I *didn't* try my best. As for why I focused on striking your left side, I'd noticed your left leg was injured."

"What was that?!" There was a flurry of shouts from the captains and the vice-captains. They shot daggers at me, looking like they wanted to tear me limb from limb.

Eeek! I'm sorry for debasing chivalry and attacking your beloved knight captain's weak spot!

"What made you think my left leg was injured?" Saviz asked.

"Huh? Um, well...when you walked, you moved your right leg faster than your left. When you stood, you balanced your weight more towards your right side. An experienced knight like you would normally have perfect posture, so I figured there had to be a reason for it."

The captains and vice-captains went quiet. They were all staring at me now, wide-eyed.

Huh? Wh-what did I do this time?

"I see. Fia Ruud..." He raised his hand. "I'll remember your name." And immediately, the announcer called the ceremony to a close.

A Tale of the
Secret Saint

Saviz, Captain of the Knight Brigades

MY NAME IS SAVIZ NÁV, captain of the Náv Black Dragon Knights. I became captain ten years ago at the young age of seventeen. Normally, one so young could never rise to such a position...but as I was the younger brother of the king, no one dared object.

To be the captain was to shoulder a great burden. As the leader of the knight brigades, I was responsible for the lives of all knights under my command. A single faulty decision could lead to the deaths of many, but how to balance that against the fact that not all lives can be saved? My position required the composure to remain calm in the heat of battle, to find the outcome with minimal loss.

"Minimal loss." Easy words to say when I wasn't the knight being sacrificed. Would that knight feel the same?

No. No, I mustn't falter. I mustn't doubt, mustn't ask for forgiveness.

To dispel all fear and doubt from my knights, I must stand, ever composed, at the helm.

The skies were clear on the day of the welcome ceremony. I'd heard good things about this year's recruits, and I was looking forward to finally seeing them for myself.

I entered the ceremony grounds and stepped onto the platform. The new recruits looked up at me starry-eyed, as they did every welcome ceremony. They were young and still full of dreams and aspirations, joining the knight brigade out of adoration for the ideals of that noble profession.

So long as you remember those dreams and aspirations, you'll become splendid knights.

I finished my address and looked over the recruits again. Among the mass of exuberated knights, only one looked back at me calmly.

Who was that? She didn't allow herself to be swept along by the exhilarated knights around her, instead remaining calm and analyzing the situation. An attitude suited to command.

I descended from the platform and summoned the knight in charge of testing.

"There was only one female recruit with red hair, sir. Fia of the Ruud knight family, assigned to the First Knight Brigade."

"I assume she was chosen for the First Knight Brigade because of...*that.*"

"That's correct, sir."

The First Knight Brigade, in charge of guarding the royal family, had required more young female knights lately. And the one chosen just happened to be *her*. How interesting.

"Have her do the exhibition match...and I'll be her opponent."

"I'm...sorry?" The knight looked at me blankly for a good ten seconds. They didn't show it on the surface, but they were surely panicking on the inside. "I-I mean you no disrespect, sir, but she's just a recruit! She is by no means a match for you, the strongest of all the knights! And a captain has never participated in the exhibition matches before!"

"True. But I intend to see for myself if she is worthy of guarding *her*. I'm sure the church would be happier if the young guard was personally tested by me, no?"

"O-oh, of course! Forgive me for not understanding your intent. It was foolish of me!"

There was nothing to understand; I made all that up just now. I just want to try crossing swords with this girl, this knight who shows such promise.

Sometimes I tired of being captain, of needing a good reason for every single thing I did.

The first thing I noticed when I came face-to-face with Fia Ruud was how small she was. She was quite a bit shorter than your average female knight.

So why do I sense the same intensity I feel when fighting captain-class knights? Either I was losing my edge or there was something more to her than met the eye.

"My name is Fia Ruud! It is an honor to receive your guidance!"

she declared in a high-pitched voice befitting a girl her age. She approached...and, once she was five meters away, she leapt forward. The girl drew her sword at a speed the likes of which I'd never seen and swung at my left. I blocked—her sword was much heavier than it looked. What *was* that thing?

Fia retreated momentarily before dashing back in, swinging down on my left, left, left, and then left again. The last blow was particularly powerful—I pushed her sword back on reflex alone.

Just what in the world is this girl? Or...no, perhaps it's her sword?

I checked the blade: it was a magic sword enhanced with multiple effects. Enhanced swords were rare, valuable, and impossible to manufacture. Most of those rare swords only held one enhancement, but this one? It held both a speed and an attack enhancement, as well as a Veil cast to hide them both. But what really interested me was the strength of the enhancements themselves.

I called Cyril over to test the blade and discovered that it was a magic sword of similar power to our national treasures. I'd have to double-check with the Third Mage Knight Brigade, but I was certain the speed and attack enhancements were at least +300—on par with equipment from the Golden Age.

When pressed, she said she received the magic sword from her father, Vice-Captain Dolph. I didn't quite buy it, but Dolph himself supported her story. Abandoning this useless line of questioning, I tried another.

"One last question: during the exhibition match, why did you focus on attacking my left side?" Most knights would've attacked from my right side to take advantage of my blind spot, or at least balanced it out more between both sides. Her persistent focus on my left was unnatural.

"It's because I have my chivalry as a knight, sir. I would never take advantage of your blind side, especially not when you were so gracious as to promise not to strike back," she answered, wearing an odd (and suspicious) expression. Despite having the eyes of a leader, the girl would still dare to lie to *me,* of all people.

And she seemed strangely proud of her answer. The corners of her mouth twitched, on the verge of breaking into a smile. I pressed for an answer once more and she gave in, admitting she aimed at my left side because of my injury.

She was right—the injury to my left ankle hadn't healed fully, lowering my guard on strikes from the left. But that was strictly confidential. The injury in question was from over ten years ago and was supposed to be known only to my captains and vice-captains. Even on record, it was officially recorded as a full recovery. Now my captains and vice-captains were up in arms, suspecting an information leak.

They were clearly wrong, given the girl's explanation: She'd analyzed my minute movements and arrived at the truth on her own.

Fascinating. Not only did she show the qualities of a leader, but she had a sharp eye for hidden truths.

A Tale of the

Secret
Saint

The First Knight Brigade

FABIAN AND I were working up a good sweat training that morning, the rhythmic clanking of our swords echoing throughout the training grounds.

"Nice strikes, Fabian," I said. "Accurate and straight. No wonder you got picked as a representative at the welcome ceremony!"

"Thank you," he said with a smile. "As for you, Fia..."

Oh? Is he going to compliment me back?

"Your sword strikes are a tad weak. I know most people credit your performance during the exhibition match to the enhancements on your sword, but I still remember the way you disarmed the examiner in the first stage. You were just using a wooden sword. It doesn't seem like you're holding back from what I've seen of you this past week. Where did that power go?"

Ack—what's this sudden interrogation?! You're supposed to return a compliment, right? "Uhhh, the truth is...I'm not much of a morning person, you know? But sword drills are always in the morning. It's a real shame."

"Fia, being a morning person doesn't explain this. C'mon."

"Well. *Well!* I also, uh...crack under pressure?"

"Fia, those are toddler-level excuses."

Lies! No way Fabian's ever even met *a three-year-old! If he had, he'd know that none of them are as articulate and very good with talking words as me!*

The real reason was that I couldn't use Invigorate for long periods of time without giving myself major muscle pain the next day.

"*Pfft!* Oh, Fia," he laughed. There I'd been, mulling over my response, and he was just amusing himself by watching me. "Sorry, sorry! The face you make when you're all stammering and nervous is just *extremely* good. Anyway, we've got culture class today, right? Chess class?"

Despite his curiosity, Fabian was still ultimately a gentleman. He didn't push too hard and overlooked anything unusual about me. Sure, we were both new recruits, but he seemed pretty knightly already if you asked me!

I returned my wooden sword to where I found it and smiled back at him. "Thank you, Fabian. Gotta change first, but I'll meet you in the recreation room in a few."

It'd been a full week since I was assigned to the First Knight Brigade—the brigade in charge of protecting the royal family. That pretty much meant the King and the captain. They were guarded in shifts of three by a good score of knights, though there were more people in the brigade than needed just for guard duty. For that reason, newly assigned knights were generally exempt from guard duty and given special First Knight Brigade training instead.

That training included learning etiquette, dance, the common continental language, music, poetry...

Ugh, just on and on! When will a knight even use this stuff?! Yeah, I have memories from being a royal princess, sure, but that was over three hundred years ago. What little boring stuff I even remember, it's gotta be outdated by a few centuries! And now I have to relearn most of this stuff from scratch? Fun, fun. I suppose guarding royalty means you need to know a bunch of oddball skills, but these classes really suck.

The other new knights look thrilled to do horseback riding practice and sword drills—our standard training—but I think they feel the same about the cultural lessons. Totally miserable.

Speaking of new knights, there were twenty if you included me and Fabian. Of that twenty, ten were female—which was strange, considering the low overall ratio of females to males in the knight brigades.

Fabian mentioned that the King was incapable of loving a woman, Maybe it's because he's kinda sexist, and this is some way to overcome it? Yeah, a kind of exposure therapy for women. That made sense, didn't it? Or maybe...

Maybe the captain's tired of being surrounded by men all the time and wanted a change of pace? The adoration the male knights had for the captain must've been really overbearing; I could see him wanting to get away from that for a bit.

Pondering the possibilities, I finished slipping into new clothes and made my way to the recreation room.

A chill ran up my spine as I reached the door. *He wouldn't be here again today, would he?* I thought, and timidly opened the door. Immediately a voice called my name.

"There you are, Fia. Took your sweet time, didn't you? C'mon, I already lined up the pieces."

"*Eek!* Captain Desmond!" *I knew I shouldn't have opened the door...*

"Come sit down. You're playing white."

Sitting comfortably in the seat farthest back was Desmond, captain of the Second Knight Division. Handsome and friendly with hair of navy blue, he described himself as a thirty-two-year-old bachelor still living in the knight dormitory. With his personable attitude, he and First Knight Brigade Captain Cyril were considered pillars of the Knight Brigade—"the Dragon and the Tiger."

"Um, sir," I offered, "I'm flattered you always make time to play chess with me, but shouldn't you be working?" *Get lost, man!* I wanted to say, but...well, you know. He was a captain.

I think he got my intent but chose to ignore it. Instead, he beckoned me to sit down across from him. "It's fine! We captains don't actually have set tasks to do; we only work when something comes up. The most important thing is that we remain easy to find.

THE FIRST KNIGHT BRIGADE

Which means I actually *have* to stay here; I told my subordinate I'd be in the recreation room for the next hour or so, see?"

"Oh. Is that right?" It didn't seem like I could worm my way out of this, so I sat down across from him.

I'll admit, though, that chess with Desmond was all right. We chatted as we played.

"White first," he said. "Now...how goes it? Getting used to the knight life?"

"Yes, everyone's been very accommodating. I'd still like to finish with all the training and get assigned something soon, though." It was a pretty run-of-the-mill answer from a recruit. I moved a center pawn forward.

"Ha ha! I bet. They say the First Knight Brigade has to learn some pretty odd things. Poetry and the like."

"Yes, we had poetry just the other day with 'to honor thy lady' as a theme. Fabian really got into it with this wonderful poem—the kind of stuff that makes you think he's gonna be a real womanizer one of these days."

"Ah, that guy. He seems like the popular sort. You joined at the same time, right? A wonderful poet, a womanizer...are you interested?" Desmond looked up at me.

I laughed. "Oh no, he's the son of a marquess. Our social statuses are much too far apart."

"True, true. Of course, it'd be a different thing if you had some kind of edge, wouldn't it? A special ability, perhaps."

"Heh. Yeah, something so great that if I shoot them a wink, and they'll drop to one knee and write me poetry, right?"

"Heck of an image, there. You've got some imagination."

We exchanged such small talk as we played, jabbing back and forth. To tell you the truth, I had no idea why he played chess with me. He had to be busy, whatever excuses he made for being here. On my first day of chess class, he just sat there waiting for me like an old friend. Ever since then, he'd been my opponent.

Most knights rarely got a chance to even speak with a captain, so I was worried my colleagues would be jealous, thinking it was favoritism. When I asked Fabian for his input, he just looked at me funny.

"You realize you fought the captain, right? If somebody's going to be jealous of you, it's going to be about *that*. Even then, I doubt anyone will be jealous. The knight brigades are a strict hierarchy, after all. No respectable knight would dare question a superior...but I guess you never know. People do strange things out of jealousy. Maybe keep an eye out, eh?"

How helpful, Fabian.

"Oh, right," said Desmond, shaking me back to the present. "I heard you'll be doing monster extermination with the Sixth Knight Brigade tomorrow. Take care."

"Thank you, will do."

We continued the small talk over a few more games. In the end, I had four victories and one loss. Desmond really fluctuated between strong days and weak days. Today happened to be a weak day for him...unless he was just giving me free wins for good luck tomorrow.

The First Secret Meeting of the Captains

T HAT NIGHT, three knights gathered for a secret meeting in the captain and vice-captain's recreation room.

The elegance of the room made it clear that it was for the elites of the organization. The flooring was black walnut wood, dark-indigo material that made a satisfying sound when shoes clacked against it. Towards the back of the room were chessboards and billiard tables, with tables and chairs placed a distance away. All these items were of the finest quality.

Cyril, captain of the First Knight Brigade, sat in a luxurious velvet chair. He turned to the man next to him. "So? How was my new recruit?"

Desmond, captain of the Second Knight Brigade, swirled the contents of a glass in one hand. "Difficult to read."

Unsatisfied, Cyril pressed further. "You're telling me that you—the head of the military police—couldn't get a read on her?! You've played chess with her three times already; you should have figured her out long before now!"

"Calm down. That cool captain facade of yours is slipping."

"Calm down? *Me*? You're asking the most bloodthirsty man in the organization to *calm down*? Spare me, Desmond."

"No need to sound so proud of yourself. As for Fia, she's a sort I've never seen before." Desmond gulped down the amber contents of his glass before placing it on the counter and ordering another from the server.

Desmond was captain of the Second Knight Brigade and the highest authority in charge of the Royal Castle's defense. He was also the commandant of the military police, a group with members in every brigade. The military police investigated not just the internal affairs of the knight brigade but also trespassers in the Royal Castle and suspicious people in the general population.

Beneath Desmond's friendly demeanor beat the heart of a master interrogator, the soul of a torturer who held nothing back when it came time to squeeze confessions from captured spies and suspects.

"Have you ever wondered," Desmond mused, "why all the best torture devices are given female names like the 'Duke Jungwald's Daughter' or the 'Iron Maiden'? I have a theory. You see, it's always women who bring calamity. The tools bring truth. The words of women, on the other hand...worthless."

"Hold on, Desmond. Are you still sore about your fiancée? She left you and married your little brother. Dreadful business, of course, but isn't it about time to move on?"

"Oh, shove it! You don't understand how it feels!" Desmond snatched his drink from the server and downed it all at once.

"Back on topic—Fia is a special type. Our chess games are a fine example. When I play a strong game, she loses. That much is normal. When I play a weak game, though, she always ekes out a win."

"What does that matter?" Cyril asked.

"Typically, one's own strength doesn't change. If your opponent is far weaker than you, you should always win by a large margin. But Fia always barely won no matter how weakly I played."

"Hmph. Interesting."

"She seemed shocked when I pointed it out, so I can only assume she does it unconsciously. She's reading her opponent's strength and adjusting her own to win by the narrowest margin, as if by habit. As for why or how, I can't figure it out for the life of me."

"I'm shocked," said Cyril. "Frankly, this is the first time I've seen you unable to read someone."

"She noticed the captain's old leg injury, which should've been near impossible, and she did it in a moment with almost no information. It's abnormal. But now I'm monitoring her, and what do I find? The girl's not perceptive in the slightest. She didn't even notice Fabian's haircut. How do you not notice someone you deal with every day cutting their hair by three centimeters?! She's clearly as thick-headed as it gets...usually."

"So, from what I understand, she reads her opponent's strength when fighting and aims for a narrow win. And yet she's normally unperceptive, except when it comes to injuries. Just what in the world is she?"

"Precisely what I'm asking..." Emptying his third drink, Desmond ordered two more of the same. "How are things on your end, Enoch?"

The man with light-purple hair looked up from his drink and nodded. He was a refined-looking man, and his almond-shaped eyes were alight with intelligence. He seemed like the sort who could comprehend all the phenomena of this world...but that was completely untrue. In fact, his skull was packed with nothing but magic. He was Enoch, captain of the Third Mage Knight Brigade.

"Our analysis of the sword confirms that it has variable enhancement effects, effects thought lost after the Golden Age. The attack and speed enhancements on the sword seem to increase in proportion to the wielder's own strength."

"Truly?!" Desmond exclaimed. "Then it's really as powerful as the national treasures?"

"There are only three known items with variable enhancements in the kingdom," Enoch continued, "and all of them have been safely passed down through the royal bloodline for the last three hundred years. So why has such a sword appeared now?"

"Dolph said it was from his family's treasury," said Desmond, "but not even a hundred years have passed since the Ruuds became a knight family. How could they have obtained a treasure from three hundred years ago?"

"Dolph's and Fia's testimonies did line up," said Cyril said, "didn't they?"

Desmond frowned. "Yeah, I checked them both myself. They aren't lying." He ran his fingers through his hair, a habit of his when it was time to rack his brain. "This all feels wrong. We're missing something. A piece of the puzzle that answers every question ..."

"Perhaps we lack the context to even know what to *look* for," said Cyril. "Regardless, you can stop meeting with Fia now. There's no point in probing further. She's my brigade's recruit and therefore my responsibility."

"Sure. I don't see any point in asking her more questions either," said Desmond. "She's kind of a letdown, don't you think? She claimed that attacking the captain's weakness was chivalrous. You'd *think* that would leave us with a real malicious little monster to expose, but she's as simple and honest as can be."

"You don't need to sound so disappointed," said Cyril. "And, by the way, no more shadowing Fia either."

"Hey, I was just doing my job! You make me sound like a stalker or something when you put it like that!"

The two knights bickered all throughout the night while a third calmly enjoyed his drink.

A Tale of the
Secret
Saint

Monster Extermination

*A*T LAST, *time to exterminate some monsters!*

I was in high spirits that morning. Monster extermination was a big part of the knight brigades' job, and no matter where you were assigned, you'd eventually end up doing it sometime in your first year.

Today, Fabian and I were to join the Sixth Knight Brigade, which specialized in monster extermination. We were fresh recruits without any real combat experience, so our role was just to watch and learn from our seniors. Barring special circumstances, there'd be no fighting on our part.

We split into five units of twenty, with Fabian and me in Unit Three. Our destination was Starfall Forest, about an hour north of the royal capital by horse.

As I rode in the back of Unit Three, I felt a wave of nostalgia come over me. The towns and cities might have changed in the past three hundred years, but the forest hadn't. Starfall Forest was the forest closest to the royal capital, and I'd visited it from time to time in my past life.

Upon reaching the forest, we split into our five units and received a quick explanation from our unit leaders. We were then each handed a small vial containing a sparkling liquid—a healing potion.

Ten of us would fight monsters, five would guard the saints, two would scout for monsters, and Fabian and I would be joined by one other knight to patrol in between as a precaution.

You read that right—the saints were here. I hadn't so much as seen a saint in this life yet, so I was really looking forward to meeting one. But even after we finished preparing, received our explanations, and set off, I still hadn't seen a single saint. Even weirder, the knights lined up in rows, like they were waiting for something to happen. The saints couldn't have not arrived yet... could they?

After thirty minutes of waiting, five horse-drawn coaches arrived at the entrance of the forest. From the carriages stepped fifteen women in white robes. The highest-ranking knight present, Vice-Captain Guy, quickly moved to greet them. The remainder of the knights put their right fists across their hearts and lowered their heads—the knight salute. I quickly followed suit.

"Thank you for coming, Your Graces. I am Guy, vice-captain of the Sixth Brigade. It is a pleasure to make your acquaintance."

The saints gave a casual nod to Guy and followed him. After that, each unit was assigned three saints. The three saints assigned to Unit Three must've been roughly in their twenties, thirties, and forties, respectively. Apparently, it was normal for them not to introduce themselves, instead choosing to be addressed as "Her Grace". Although, apparently the ten most powerful saints were referred to as First Saint, Second Saint, Third Saint, etc., ordered from strongest downward, and *their* names were known throughout the realm.

"Thank you for joining us today, Your Graces." Hector, our unit's leader, greeted the saints.

The white robes of the saints came down to just below their knees to overlap with their high-laced boots, and each wielded a staff imbued with a magic stone. They nodded wordlessly back at Hector before each giving their staff to a nearby knight.

Um, what? Is that supposed to be a sign of trust? Or are the staves heavy, so they're making the knights carry them? I wasn't sure which weird possibility was true until I noticed the way the saints didn't so much as give the knights a single word or a glance.

It was definitely the latter.

After that, we entered the forest with our unit.

I immediately felt bad for the knights assigned to guard the saints. There were branches everywhere in the forest, and they had to chop away every single one to keep them from even gently scraping the saints' bodies. Then the saints would walk down the cleared path without so much as a thanks for all that effort.

Hmm...I guess people's values have changed in the past three hundred years? I wasn't arrogant enough to insist things stay the same forever, but these particular changes really irked me.

"Contact!" the knight walking at the front suddenly yelled.

A boar-type monster appeared—it was a violet boar, a two-meter-long beast known for being extremely aggressive.

It bared its tusks at us and huffed.

The knights assigned to kill the monsters quickly circled around the beast, seamlessly dividing into decoys and attackers. Cut by cut, they gradually wore the violet boar down...but then, something odd happened.

The saints just...walked away from the scene of the fight and sat themselves down on a flat boulder.

Huh? The three saints started making small talk, completely disregarding the fight right next to them. The five guards assigned to protecting them circled around them, forming a secure perimeter.

Um...what is *this? I thought saints were supposed to participate in battles and be on standby to heal any knight on the spot. Was I wrong?*

I stared absently at the saints until, after not much time at all, the monster was slain. A single injured knight walked before the saints, and all three of them placed their hands over his injury and whispered a spell. After about thirty seconds, a white glow enveloped the injury, and they removed their hands to reveal that the wound had closed completely. The knight bowed over and over before he was finally overwhelmed by emotion, falling to his knees and crying out in gratitude.

The saints themselves simply wiped the sweat from their brows and listened as the knight went on and on, seeming satisfied with their work.

Um, the knight's arm was injured, I suppose. I did see what looked like bite marks, and I think a tusk pierced his arm, but it was a light injury. It shouldn't have taken spells like that—it should've been fixed in seconds!

Oh. Oh, wow...umm, I knew the power of the saints had dwindled, but are they really this weak now?!

I was in my own world for a while after my big discovery, and I only snapped out of it when Fabian told me it was lunchtime. I took my lunch, which had been carefully preserved in a giant leaf, and sat by his side.

"Fabian..."

"Yes, Fia?"

"Um...the saints are really amazing, aren't they? I mean, they closed up that knight's wound in just thirty seconds. That's incredible, right?" Hopefully Fabian would say I was wrong and would tell me that those three were apprentices or something. Full-fledged saints were far more impressive.

But he didn't. Instead he agreed wholeheartedly, unaware of how it made me feel. "Indeed. It's nothing short of a miracle. The saints are a blessing upon this world."

"I...see."

He looked at my face, worried. "Fia...are you crying?" I couldn't stop the tears from welling up. Fabian reached into his pocket and offered me a handkerchief. "Are you okay?"

I clung to him and cried. He wrapped his arms around me as teardrops ran messily down my cheeks.

What had happened? I was so proud to call myself a saint in my past life, always putting myself in harm's way to stand with my allies. The knights would be my shield, and I theirs. But somewhere along the way, the very definition of sainthood was twisted. Here I was, the former Great Saint, and...had nothing been left behind for those that came after me?

Fabian just let me cry in his arms. "Are you feeling okay, Fia?" he asked after a time. "Did the monster startle you? Or did just seeing the saints move you so?"

"Um...neither. My eyes are just a little bit leaky. That's all..."

"I see...then why don't you tell me where that leak is? I'll fix it up next time, eh?"

He's so kind. I promised myself I'd repay the favor in kind if the roles were ever reversed. But for now, I just unfolded the giant leaf and took a bite out of the rice ball inside.

"Oh! I thought the rice balls would be all sloppy from my tears, but...they're salted just right."

Fabian didn't say another word for the rest of our lunch. I think it was out of consideration for me.

He really is a gentleman.

We continued walking the forest after lunch, eliminating any monsters we came across. The most common monsters were those violet boars, and we finished five of them before the day was over.

"It'll be a meat festival tonight!" one knight happily exclaimed. They all seemed fond of meat. I shared the sentiment.

As for the saints, they acted the same as before—relaxing a distance away from the fight and providing healing afterwards. It wasn't until just past noon that they said their first words.

"Can we stop now?" they asked Hector, our unit leader. "We're tired."

"Understood! Let us return at once!"

And just like that, we were on our way back.

The path back was quicker. We didn't pursue any monsters unless they actually blocked our way. I noticed the knights around me begin to relax—a worrying sign. Disaster tended to strike when one was least prepared.

"Monster fast approaching!" barked the leader of the scouts. He was an attack magic user, which let him to use detection magic to sense nearby monsters.

"Wh-what?!" Hector shouted. "What direction is—"

And Hector went flying.

I took a deep breath and looked.

A deer-like monster with blue eyes glared at me, a mere three meters away. It was a flower-horned deer—a monster with antlers that spread like a flower as it grew, native only to Starfall Forest. It was a B-rank monster, the kind that surely required thirty knights to defeat. It was vastly superior to anything we'd come across so far.

B-rank monsters should've only inhabited the deep reaches of the forest, a day's travel away or farther. Our unit was woefully unprepared to deal with one. There were only twenty of us. Worse, our leader was knocked unconscious before the battle even began.

No way was *that* a coincidence—B-rank monsters were known to be intelligent. It must've targeted the one giving orders to leave us helpless and confused.

The knights faced the monster in a scattered half-circle, all scared stiff. Not even the second-in-command dared to move.

"Fabian!" I called out. "Can you take command?"

Fabian returned to his senses upon hearing my voice and blinked in confusion. "Uh...but I've never seen that monster before. I can't give orders if I don't know what it can do."

Figures. It's a monster native only within the depths of this one forest. Most people don't know anything about it.

The other knights began returning to their senses—perhaps our voices jarred them out of their stupor. They drew their blades, and...stopped. They could only stare back at the monster, unsure of what attacks it could make.

"Eeeeeek!" The three saints suddenly shrieked and scattered in the opposite direction.

"Wait, don't run!" I yelled. The flower-horned deer instinctively chased moving targets.

Without stopping to think, I drew my sword and moved to intercept the monster just as it started after them.

"Invigorate: Attack x3; Speed x3!" My blade met the antlers as it charged. "Ngh!" The impact pushed me back a little, but I still blocked it. "Guys, I have experience fighting flower-horned deer! Follow my lead!"

I stared into the monster's blue eyes and held my ground. Seconds later, its eyes suddenly turned red.

"Get back!" At once, flames erupted in a three-meter radius around the monster.

"Wh-what?! It's burning?"

"It's dangerous, get back!"

The knights retreated.

"Watch the eyes!" I called out. "You have to watch the eyes of a flower-horned deer! Attack when its eyes turn blue; pull back when they're red!" I knew that it could only control fire when its eyes were red, but it also couldn't rush you in that state. "The monster's hide is tough! It'll take time to kill."

I turned to Fabian and called out, "Fabian, blow your emergency whistle and call for backup! It's B-rank—we need more people!"

Immediately, Fabian and all the other knights blew their emergency whistles. Now we just had to pray that there was another unit nearby. There was no way a single, leaderless unit could manage alone.

The flower-horned deer's flames should recede soon...

"We need three people to block the antlers with shields! The rest of you circle around! This monster is quick—don't leave any gaps or it'll break through our line and pick us off one by one!"

The well-trained knights responded at once and began to encircle the flower-horned deer.

"Aim your attacks at the white abdomen! Its back is too hard to cut!"

Minutes passed. We struggled against it, still unable to pierce its thick hide, when an out-of-place, nonchalant voice called out to us.

"Oh? I came when I heard the whistle, but I didn't expect this..."

I turned, and there he was: the knight known as the Dragon.

Cyril, Captain of the First Knight Brigade

M Y NAME IS Cyril Sutherland, captain of the First Knight Brigade. I also bear the title of duke, having inherited it from my father at the age of seventeen, ten years ago.

My father was the younger brother of the last king, making me second in line to the throne after Captain Saviz. Perhaps inspired by that, Desmond and I were called "the Dragon and the Tiger"—Desmond being the Tiger, and I the Dragon. But that title irked me. The dragon was emblazoned upon the royal family's coat of arms, after all. Even the word "dragon" itself often referred to the king. Although I was second in line to the throne, using the moniker "Dragon" for myself seemed disrespectful.

But when I brought up my concerns to the captain, he seemed utterly unbothered. "One day, you may be the heir. Don't scorn the title of Dragon."

There are some things in this world that we are helpless against, things beyond our control despite our talent and no matter our efforts. That lesson was carved in blood ten years ago, when the captain lost his right eye...and his emotions. I was helpless to stop it. And so I swore from that day onward to be his new eye. I kept a watchful gaze over everything important to him, removed all that was not fit for his sight, and vowed to be his right hand in battle.

I gave my entire being to the kingdom.

But I would spare nothing for him, my future king.

I accompanied the captain on a training exercise to the nearby forest, with fifty guards. Though he practiced the sword every day at the Royal Castle's training grounds, every so often he wanted real combat practice. As for why, I could only guess. Perhaps he sought even greater strength than he already possessed. Maybe he merely wanted to dispel his lethargy...or there was something weighing on his mind and he wanted to work through his thoughts with the shedding of blood.

We had hunted ten monsters in about two hours. The beasts were merely C-rank, and so, as always, the captain handled them alone.

He effortlessly cut through yet another monster, its blood sticking to his sword. Could this bring him some sort of peace? Or...

An emergency whistle pierced the silence. I recognized the tone: a Knight Brigade's emergency whistle. This forest was under the Sixth Knight Brigade's jurisdiction, so something must have happened to them.

The captain took the lead and made his way towards the sound. Just a few minutes later, we found a Sixth Knight Brigade unit as expected, but there was something...surprising.

For the briefest of moments, I froze. There was a flower-horned deer, a B-rank monster normally found in the depths of the forest—but that wasn't what shocked me. No, it was the new recruit from my brigade, standing at the center of the fight giving orders.

The new recruit was the first to turn and address me. "Captain Cyril! We're up against a flower-horned deer! We have it surrounded in an enclosure, down to eighty-five percent of its 450 units of health! Its flames extinguish seven seconds after its eyes turn blue!"

"Huh...?" From a young age, I was taught to speak with clarity and elegance. Today, for what was perhaps the first time in my life, I sounded positively boorish.

How did she know so much about the flower-horned deer, a monster found only in this forest? How was she able to quantify the monster's health? I couldn't even check if she was right or not—I'd never heard of anyone able to measure such a thing. And how did she know the timing of the monster's eye color change so exactly? Such a thing was impossible...wasn't it?

"Fia..." I said with a weary sigh. "You're even more of a surprise than this monster."

She just smiled back at me happily. "I didn't expect to see you here either! And thank you for coming to our rescue! We can rest easy now that you're here!"

Not...what I meant. Feeling incredibly drained, I returned to my usual place to the right of the captain. He stepped towards the monster, and Fia finally noticed him.

"Huh?! The captain's here?!" This girl...was she really as perceptive as she seemed sometimes? Perhaps Desmond was right—maybe she was brilliant at analysis but as dull as it got in other ways.

But how could she miss a presence as strong as the captain's? Is her analysis so perfect that she's discovered...our secret? Is that why she didn't even register the captain's presence? No, surely not...

I changed my focus to the monster before me. The instant the flames cleared away, the captain drew his sword and sliced the head off the charging monster in one quick motion.

The knights clamored excitedly...

"Whoa..."

"The captain just slew that monster we were struggling with like it was nothing!"

But such a sight was normal to me. The captain was strong. I knew that well.

I left the cleanup of the monster's body to the knights and focused on more urgent concerns. "Fia, come here."

"Yes, sir!"

Fabian looked on with eyes of pity, already able to guess why I'd called her over.

But Fia herself was all smiles, seeming perfectly clueless. "Captain Cyril, thank you for saving us!" she said with a wide grin.

The captain sighed, confounded by her carefree attitude.

Fia quickly turned to him and, completely misunderstanding his sigh, exclaimed, "Ah, n-no, I mean, thank you for coming, Captain Cyril! And thank *you* for defeating the monster, Captain Saviz!"

The captain looked at me with a raised brow.

Forgive me, sir. As her superior, I accept full responsibility for her stupidity.

A Tale of the
Secret
Saint

13
Healing Potion

*S*AVIZ BEHEADED *a B-rank monster in just one strike like it was nothing... Amazing! I wonder what kind of training I'd have to do to get that good...*

I was thinking about that when Cyril called for me. He glanced down at my arm in surprise. "Fia, you're hurt?!"

"Huh? Ohhh. Yeah, I was grazed a bit by the flower-horned deer's antlers. It's just a scratch, though."

"A scratch? That has to be at least ten centimeters long." He rolled up my sleeves to check the wound. "It looks deep too. Go show it to the..." His voice tapered off. I followed his eyes to see the saints from earlier yelling at the knights. We were out of earshot range, but it was clear what they were angry about.

Knights had to be flexible and respond to new situations the right way. Sometimes, that meant abandoning your given role in an emergency. So when the flower-horned deer appeared, the saints' guards had to join with the rest of the knights to take it down—otherwise, the entire unit would've been wiped out.

But the saints were clearly offended that they'd been abandoned, and now they were chewing the knights out. Honestly, I was glad I was out of hearing range.

There was no chance they'd heal me. I could see quite a few injured people being denied.

I turned back to Cyril. "It's just a scratch. We were given some healing potions, so I'll drink mine later."

"No, drink it now. It takes some time to work. The sooner you drink it, the better."

Jeez...but healing from a potion really hurts! I'll just heal myself later—I am *a former Great Saint after all. Heh heh...*

"Fia...? You're not avoiding drinking it because of the pain, are you?" asked Cyril. "It'll only cause you more trouble down the road if you don't, so act your age and drink it!" He grabbed me by the base of my chin and tried to force my mouth open.

"S-s-sir, please! We Ruuds are a sturdy bunch! Oh! In fact, my father said only weaklings rely on healing potions, and as a daughter of the Ruud family, I need to uphold my family's val—*blrghghgrh*!" Cyril forced the contents of a healing potion down my throat mid-speech.

I reflexively covered my mouth with both hands as a bitter taste spread across my tongue. *"Aieee!* It's *(bleh!)* so *(gack!)* bitter! Ugh!" I looked around me, desperate to find a way to deal with the taste, and saw Saviz. I gave him a pleading look, but he only waved at me, amused.

Don't just wave, help me out! I started jumping in place. *It's so bitter, bitter, bitterrrrr! Ah, my tongue won't stop throbbing! Aw, I should've trained by eating bitter stuff just to avoid this!*

My thoughts were getting a little incoherent as I jumped up and down...until my mind suddenly stumbled upon a good idea. *Something sweet! Yeah, that'll erase the bitterness!*

Restless, I scanned the area and found what I was looking for—a tree. I bolted towards it.

"Wha—hey, where are you going?" Cyril called out, worry in his voice. I ignored him.

The branches of the tree were heavily laden with red fruits the size of my thumb. I grabbed some and immediately tossed them into my mouth.

"Hey, spit that out!" Cyril said, but too late; I'd already swallowed them. The fruit was super sweet, as expected. I'd always wondered why the forest animals didn't eat them.

"Fiaaaa!" Cyril finally caught up with me and thrust his fingers inside my mouth, searching around for the fruit—but he found nothing.

"Dith chu wanth to eath too? There'sh more, buh pleash find yhour ohn inshtead oh taking it fromh muh mouth."

He pulled his fingers out of my mouth. "You're...okay? Those fruits may look all right, but they're far more bitter than any healing potion."

"Huh? But...they're sweet, though." I tilted my head quizzically, frantically grabbing a second handful, and then a third, tossing them one by one into my mouth. "Mmm! So *sweet!*"

"Hmm...I doubt there's anything wrong with your sense of taste if you can taste healing potions." Cyril gingerly grabbed a fruit off the tree, took a bite, and— "*Ngh!* I was a fool to trust you..." He fell to his knee with a pained expression.

Wow. He looked so elegant, even with his face all contorted. I was a little jealous. "Are you not good with sweet foods?"

"What are you talking about? There's nothing sweet about this!"

"Huh? There's nothing wrong with not liking sweets, you know? You can admit it." I tossed a few more into my mouth. Cyril's gaze was piercing. "You want more after all? Here."

I picked another fruit and held it out to him, but he just slinked back like he was repulsed by it.

That was odd, I thought.

A moment later, Saviz walked up to me.

"Oh, sir! Would you like one? They're very good."

He stared at me for a few seconds before slowly reaching out, taking the fruit from my extended palm, and eating it whole.

"Sir!" exclaimed Cyril, but Saviz chewed the fruit regardless.

"It's sweet..."

"What? Impossible!" Surprised, Cyril plucked another and took a nibble, only to groan and drop to the ground again. I was surprised he didn't just spit it out, but I guess he was too refined to do something so crass.

Observing Cyril, Saviz plucked a fruit of his own and took a bite. "Fia, why don't *you* grab a fruit, then give it to Cyril?"

"Yes, sir. Here."

Cyril gingerly took the fruit from my extended hand and ate it whole. He grimaced as he bit down on it, but his eyes darted open a moment later. "It's sweet..."

Oh, I see how it is. Cyril would only take a small bite when I offered it, but he ate it whole when Saviz told him to. He really does adore Saviz. I'm...only a little offended. Just a little!

"Yes, yes, it's sweet," I said. "But it's okay, some people think men who can't handle sweet things are actually cool!"

"What is this?" Cyril asked Saviz, ignoring my words of comfort. *Rude!*

"According to legend, there used to be spirits dwelling in this forest who would give their divine favor to those they loved. Fia, you must be one of those blessed by the spirits. Those spirits are changing this bitter fruit sweet for you. Or perhaps, if the spirits are indeed gone from this forest, the forest itself has come to your aid. But it's unfortunate... I'm sure you would have made a splendid saint if only you could use healing magic."

All girls born in the kingdom were tested to see if they could use healing magic at the age of three, and again at ten. Those who could use healing magic were taken in by the church. Anyone not taken, like me, was assumed to lack that power.

"That's all right. I already have everything I could need." I smiled back at Saviz. Being born again in this kingdom was already the greatest blessing I could receive from the spirits.

There was silence for a few moments until Cyril spoke up. "Um, Fia...seeing as you're settled down now, I'd like to ask you a few questions."

"Sure, what is it?" I tilted my head, wondering what he wanted to ask. It was at that moment my entire body was assailed by sharp pain.

"Aaagh!"

I forgot—I drank a healing potion!

"Fia?!" Cyril yelled, seeing me suddenly drop to the ground, but I was in no state to reply.

It hurts, it hurts, it hurts, it hurts, it hurts, it hurts, it hurts, it hurts, it hurts, it hurts, it hurts! This healing potion...it's off. Made wrong. Has to be! No wonder Zavilia attacked me if it hurt this bad. Zavilia...what's Zavilia doing right now? Ah, shoot, my brain's a wreck. A wreck? Who the heck made this wreck of a healing potion?!

Seeing me writhe in pain on the ground, Cyril sadly muttered, "You must be one of those people who has a bad reaction to healing potions. It must be especially strong in your case—you shrugged off that arm wound earlier, and yet..."

Well, that's not wrong, exactly. Healing potions normally just heighten one's natural restorative ability, but the one I drank was made improperly—it caused pain depending on the strength of the drinker's healing magic. Which meant I was in a world of pain.

"This is a problem," he said. "That pain will periodically return until your wound heals. It'll be hard for you to return with the Sixth Knight Brigade like this." He looked at the Sixth Knight

Brigade, nearly finished with clearing away the monster corpse, as he spoke.

"N-no, wait!" I stammered. "I have to return with the Sixth Knight Brigade... Today's meat festival day!"

"Excuse me?" Cyril replied, nonplussed.

"It's fine, okay? If I don't think about the pain, it'll go away! But if I keep thinking about the meat, I'll just feel worse!"

"Fia..." Cyril gave me a sublime smile. "Why don't you heal up, and then we'll have a nice, long talk?"

"N-no! You're just going to lecture me like Ardio does! You can't just take my meat, I worked too hard!" With great effort, I got myself up and stepped a little farther away.

O-oh...th-the pain's starting to fade!

"Look, look, I'm healed!" I cried. "It doesn't hurt anymore! I'll just be returning with the Sixth Knight Brigade now, okay?!" I was a former Great Saint, after all—I could heal an injury like that in the blink of an eye. Even that faulty healing potion's effects would only take a split second to cure. I just needed to find an opportunity to heal...

"Pardon my interruption, sir, but if I may?" Fabian cut in. "I'd be more than happy to take care of Fia, if that's all right with you. You still need to guard the captain, after all."

Cyril thought for a moment. "Indeed," he said finally. "I'll leave her in your care. There are likely more bouts of pain coming, so you may need to carry her during them. And take care not to fall behind the other knights."

He hesitated for a moment. "I've...also received a report that one of the Three Great Beasts of the continent has gone missing. The power balance in in wilderness has been upset, and monsters are leaving their usual habitats. I thought this place would be safe—it's some distance away from the missing Great Beast's territory—but I fear I was wrong. The flower-horned deer is proof enough of that. Be prepared—you may see other monsters in unusual places. Try to stay with the group."

"Understood," said Fabian with a serious look.

Thank goodness. With this, I could participate in the meat festival *and* discreetly heal myself! We met up with Unit Three, and they greeted me at once.

"Yo, Fia! Your arm's hurt? Get over here, I'll wrap it for you."

I obeyed, walking over and extending my arm, only to get my hair tousled suddenly for some reason.

"Man, that was wild! Good thing you knew what that monster was or we'd be screwed!"

"For real, that thing was nasty! Couldn't get close 'cause of the flames but couldn't back away or you'd get rammed! Tell you what, Fia, it's a good thing your timing was on point. Otherwise we'd be at the meat festival tonight, on the freakin' menu!"

"Pfft! Like hell anyone would wanna eat you!"

"Hee hee hee!" I couldn't help getting caught up in their high spirits. "Did you know the flower-horned deer tastes crazy good?" I said all smugly. "It just melts in your mouth. Like, you thought you've eaten meat before, and you take a bite? No, *that's* real meat. I bet there's gonna be a stampede to get a bite of it. Maybe even a few brawls!"

"Seriously?!"

A few of the knights were already imagining how the flower-horned deer might taste, staring at its corpse, spellbound. It was funny that they could look at this monster, alive just a few moments ago and trying to kill them, as nothing but meat now. That was knights for you.

One of the knights sloppily wrapped a bandage around my arm, and we began our return home soon after. I hadn't gotten far when I felt another intense jolt of pain throughout my body. "Khaagh!"

Shoot! I forgot about the healing potion!

"Hey, you all right, Fia?!"

"You eat somethin' bad or somethin'?"

The knights around me seemed worried. I couldn't muster a voice through the pain, so Fabian answered in my stead. "It's the aftereffects of the healing potion she used for her arm."

"Oof..."

"Yeah, that stuff sucks." The knights nodded sympathetically. I guess they knew how it felt firsthand.

Fabian picked my shield up for me. "Hmm. It'll hurt you if I carry you on my back with your armor in the way. I guess I'll just have to carry you in my arms."

And just like that, I was lifted from the ground?! *"Eek!"*

F-Fabian?! He's just...he's just doing his duty as a knight! Even if it gives me some...confusing feelings. Anyway...

"Don't trust the armor!" I sputtered. "It's, uh...cursed! So...so it feels way heavier than normal. It's not *me*, it's the armor!" Yeah, I was in horrible pain, but I had priorities: I *had* to clarify this!

"A...heavy armor curse?" Fabian mused. "I've never heard of such a thing, but it *is* you saying it, so..."

"That right?" one of the knights teased. "I didn't know they handed out cursed equipment. How convenient!"

I noticed the knights grinning at me but decided to ignore them. They were kind enough to leave it at that, at least.

My pain eventually subsided, and I had Fabian put me down. We later stopped to rest, and I took the opportunity to hide behind a tree and heal myself. Both my arm wound and the recurring pains only took an instant to heal.

All that, thanks to one crummy little healing potion.

14
Meat Festival

THE LONG-AWAITED meat festival was held later that night. Grills were set up outside in the courtyard by the canteen so we could see the meat being roasted right before our eyes. It wasn't just the Sixth Knight Brigade—the gatherers of the meat and the stars of the festival. No, many of the First, Second, and Fifth Knight Brigade also attended. What knight doesn't love a good hunk of meat?

And along with the mountains of meat came some good old-fashioned booze!

Of course, I was an adult now that I'd completed my coming-of-age ceremony, so I could legally drink. I grabbed a glass of an amber-colored drink and took a big ol' swig.

"Mmm..." I swirled it around and tried to look like I knew what I was talking about. "Kind of bubbly. Sharp, bitter notes. Is this, um, supposed to...taste good?" This was only my second time tasting alcohol—the first being the night of my coming-of-age ceremony.

Heh heh, I've come such a long way! Here I am, a member of the knight brigade, and I've even had alcohol! That's right: Cool Adult Fia is here to rock this party!

Feeling giddy, I downed the rest of my glass. *Pffha! Easy! Alcohol ain't nothing to me!* I grabbed another glass and downed half of it before Fabian found me.

"You all right, Fia? Your cheeks are kind of red."

"You caught me red-handed! Red...cheeked. Which is fine, by the way, because I can redden my cheeks whenever I want!" *How do I sound so cool all the time?*

Fabian chuckled. "Well, I've carried you before and I'll carry you again if you party yourself unconscious, eh? Though I wonder what excuse you'll make this time, now that you're armor's off."

"Heheh, whatever could you mean? I'm as light as a feather without my armor!" I grabbed a delicious-looking piece of meat and handed it to Fabian. "The flower-horned deer is the highlight of the night, so it won't be out for a while. But this violet boar's still pretty good. Try it."

Fabian took a bite. "Mmm, you're right. This is great!"

Good, Fabian, gooooood... Keep eating and drinking until you can't even remember how much I weighed in the morning! I grinned diabolically as I offered him a drink. Then, suddenly, I heard some clamoring near the entrance.

It was Cyril and Saviz. *Wow, I've really seen them two times!* Cyril himself rarely made appearances, but people said that Saviz was still scarcer. What bizarre luck I had—it was like I'd chanced across an SS-rank monster all over again.

I wanted to go thank them for saving us earlier, but they were soon enveloped by a swarm of knights. Guess I'd have to wait. Until then, I'd stuff my cheeks with meat and enjoy talking with Fabian.

That was the plan...until I heard that Cyril wanted to see Fabian and me.

Huh? Puzzled, Fabian and I walked over to him to find a room attached to the canteen. Gathered inside were the members of the Sixth Knight Brigade's Unit Three that I'd been part of.

Why am I getting goosebumps along my neck? It's like when Ardio was going to lecture me. Unless...

I tried to sneak behind Fabian.

"I can see you, Fia. Come forward." Cyril said.

"Oh...yes, sir." Left with no choice, I obeyed.

Cyril stood with (judging by the sash color) the Sixth Knight Brigade's captain behind him. As for Saviz, he sat quietly in a chair in the back.

What do I do? They're totally gonna chew me out, I just know it.

By Cyril's orders, all the members of Unit Three sat down in three rows of chairs. Once everyone was seated, he began to speak slowly and deliberately. "I've gathered you all here today to congratulate you on your splendid performances. Fighting against a B-rank monster without suffering a single casualty, holding your ground against it—fine work. Good job, everyone."

He laid on the compliments with a wondrous smile, but not one of the hardened knights in this room were deceived. Everyone waited nervously. The bomb was gonna drop sooner or later.

"However..." Cyril's smile gave way to a stern, cold gaze. "I couldn't *help* but *notice* that my *new recruit took command.* Perhaps one of you could tell me why such an unusual thing happened, hmm?"

And *kabooooom* goes the bomb.

Hector, our unit's leader, was sweating profusely now. "Forgive me, sir. I was struck at the start of the encounter and remained unconscious for the rest of the battle. I have no words to express my shame."

He ran away! Hector was only knocked out for, like, a second. And now he's gonna dodge all responsibility like this?!

"Is that right?" Cyril turned his gaze to the rest of the unit. "Would the rest of you mind telling me what you were thinking when you left command to my recruit?"

Silence.

"Starfall Forest," he continued, "is under the Sixth Knight Brigade's jurisdiction. Everybody should have been provided with a list of monsters for the area detailing their traits and abilities. Everybody *should* have read this list."

Silence.

"Let me ask again: if everyone has been keeping up with their studies, if everyone knows about the monsters of the forest, then *why was my recruit the one who took charge?* Hm?"

More silence. *That's seasoned knights for you. They know when to hold their tongues! Silence is golden, people...golden!*

"Oh dear, oh dear. It seems that no one is willing to answer my question. Is it because I'm an outsider to your brigade?" Cyril's voice turned monotone in a strange attempt at sadness. Then, suddenly, he smiled at me. "Oh, but surely a member of my own brigade wouldn't treat me so coldly! Right, Fia?"

"E-Eeeeeek!" *Scary! Scary smile, worse than the grumpy face.*

"F-F-Fabian, h-help..." I said feebly, looking over to my right. But Fabian looked pale as a ghost. He seemed frozen stiff. Had he even heard me?

Fabian's way out of it. I looked to my left at my last line of hope—the unit's second-in-command—only to find him locking eyes with the Sixth Knight Brigade's captain standing behind Cyril.

The Sixth Knight Brigade's captain was a man in his early forties with auburn-colored hair and a sturdy build. He had a mature, adult charm to him...*most* of the time. But right now he looked downright demonic, standing with his arms folded, staring his subordinate in the eyes. You could practically see devil horns sprouting from his head.

My unit's second-in-command couldn't help me either—he was a frog frozen by the steely gaze of a snake.

I had to face Cyril's wrath without any backup.

I forced a smile. "Ah ha...ha ha...o-of course, sir. I would be more than happy to answer any question you might have."

Oh boy...how am I going to get out of this one...?

"Then I'll start with an easy question," Cyril said, meeting my gaze with a smile.

Crap, crap, crap! I felt like he could see through me no matter what I said. I forced myself to laugh sweetly and smile back at him, cold sweat running down my neck all the while.

"How," he asked, "did you know about the flower-horned deer?"

Ooooh! That one's easy!

"I saw it in an illustrated monster reference book. I thought the flower-shaped antlers were really pretty, so I remembered it," I said proudly.

"Huh?" one of my fellow Unit Three knights spoke up, sounding surprised. "Didn't you say you had experience fighting them before?"

"Nah, I was bluffing. You guys wouldn't back me up if I said I read it in a book, you know? And anyway, it all worked out in the end, right?" I added with a smug, satisfied grin. Man, I was good at this. Sure, I *had* hunted down hundreds of flower-horned deer in my past life, but I wasn't shameless enough to take credit for that in this one. Besides, if I *did* claim to have fought a flower-horned deer before, they'd easily be able to figure out I was lying. You didn't have to investigate hard to find out that I'd never actually stepped out of my family's domain till now.

Or...oh, I *could* claim I'd fought them in my dreams. Yeah, why not? Dreams, past life—what's the difference? "Of course, I've fought many murderous monster deer in my dreams, so...you know. I figured I could take care of business."

The other knights looked at me with their jaws dropped.

"Y-you...!"

"You say it like it's easy! But you just read a book—no way you could learn all about a monster's abilities from that!"

"Yeah, most people would forget that kind of stuff right away! Even the monster list we studied was no help till you reminded us about the eyes!"

"Totally. And, like, if you *did* remember the eyes changed color, you still wouldn't know the timing when they switched!"

"What are you, some kinda tactics genius? You saw that thing for the first time today, right?!"

"Eh heh, oh man...lay off the compliments a little, guys." I squirmed a bit, my cheeks turned beet red.

"We're not complimenting you!"

Huh? Betrayal?! Were those insults all along?!

Cyril, who'd been watching quietly all this time, looked over the knights with slow, calculating purpose. "I see, I see. What I'm hearing now is that the esteemed knights of the Sixth Knight Brigade gave full command to...a fifteen-year-old recruit. And why? Because she convinced you that her daydreams were real?"

The knights fell silent at once.

Cyril looked at them sharply. Then he turned his gaze at me. "Let me get this straight: you had no real combat experience with flower-horned deer...but you *claimed* you did to take command. You then used knowledge from both a reference book and your dreams to defeat the thing. A reference book and dreams. You really believed that this was enough to take command?"

H-huh? I don't like where this is going. Better to keep quiet.

I directed my eyes toward my feet and said nothing. The silence hung in the air until it was unbearable. Finally, I took a nervous glance up at Cyril, only to find Desmond—the captain of the Second Knight Brigade—suddenly by his side. Desmond just shook his head wordlessly, while Cyril appeared deep in thought.

Hm? What's Desmond doing?

"All right, next question. How did you know the timing of when the flower-horned deer's eyes would change color? You stated its eyes would turn blue in *exactly* seven seconds. And, lo and behold, it changed. *Exactly* seven seconds later. What do you have to say to that?"

"Oh, well, I saw its eyes change many times before you arrived. I knew about the eyes beforehand, and I figured out the timing from there." He didn't look convinced, but I continued. "Um, that specific flower-horned deer's flames receded in three stages. The second-to-third stage lasted two-thirds as long as the first-to-second stage, so, by counting the first stage and calculating from there, I got seven seconds left for the interval."

Desmond shook his head again. Cyril's frown deepened. "Last question. You gave numbers for the total health and the remaining health of the monster. How were you able to figure out that information in the first place?"

"Um...well, you can look at the size and the antlers of a flower-horned deer to measure its total health. From there, you figure out what health remains in the fight by remembering what knight attacked, how many *times* they attacked, and by observing the monster's posture and perspiration. Stuff like that. I mean, it's mostly intuition and assumption, so there's a lot of margin for error."

Truth be told, determining a monster's health and remaining health was one of the fundamental skills of a saint. I'd defeated countless monsters in my past life, so at this point I could determine their health at a glance.

"What you're telling me," said Cyril, "is that you're able to approximate a monster's health simply by looking at. All of this while *also* determining how much damage a knight's attack will subtract from it. Am I correct?"

"Uh, sure." Desmond shook his head yet again. *What's going on with him? Must be nice being a captain, just shaking your head without a care in the world while someone else gets lectured—or even interrogated!*

Ugh, I'm so fed up with this!

"If what you're saying is true, then this is an incredible feat. I'll need to talk to the Fourth Monster Tamer Knight Brigade, but if we had you look at... What's wrong, Fia? Do you have something to say?"

"I do, but it'd probably anger you."

"I promise you that it won't. Speak freely."

"Nope! I'll just get lectured more for talking back to my superiors."

"I swear, Fia, that this is the end of my lecture."

"In that case," I shot back, fists clenched and voice raised, "*why* are we getting *lectured* when there's a *meat festival today*?! My butt isn't meant to be sitting in this stiff, uncomfortable chair! My hands aren't meant to be all gripping at the hem of my uniform, sweating bullets as you keep on lecturing—no, interrogating—me! These hands should be holding a lump of delicious, delicious meat and a refreshing drink!"

"Um..." Cyril blinked. "I'm...sorry?"

Saviz looked up and met my eyes. "Come to my place later, Fia," he said with a nod. "I'll treat you to some quality alcohol."

"Sir, yes, sir! I would never disobey an order!" I replied.

He looked across the Unit Three knights. "You are ignorant of the very monsters you hunt. Submit a report about the traits of the flower-horned deer and a method to combat them to Zackary later."

"Sir, yes, sir!" responded the knights.

Zackary, captain of the Sixth Knight Brigade, gave his subordinates a fearsome glare. "Thirty reports," he said. *"Per person."*

"Eeeeeeek!" The room filled with the ghastly shrieks of knights.

A most appetizing smell permeated the courtyard air. The long-awaited moment had finally arrived.

"The flower-horned deer's ready!" shouted the head chef.

I immediately bolted to line up, only to find nobody else lining with me. I looked around, confused.

The other members of Unit Three were lined up behind me. "You go first, Fia. You earned it more than anybody."

Huh?! Really? This meat's seriously good, you know?! But I wasn't about to pass up their kindness. "Thank you, everyone. Excuse me, Chef! Give me a tenderloin cut, please!" I sunk my teeth into the meat. "Mmm! Yum, yum, yum! It's hot, but it's so gooooood!"

It had all the deliciousness intrinsic to meat, brought to its highest form. Ah...surely delicious meat was the greatest joy in the world!

The other knights, starting with Unit Three, had the same meat in their hands soon after.

"Whoa...this is incredible!"

"It's so freakin' juicy that it just gushes when you bite it! So tender too!"

"The meat's so lean! I feel like I could keep eating this forever!"

Mm-hmm, you said it! I could chow down on this for another lifetime or two for sure!

In high spirits, I ate and drank with the knights of Unit Three.

"But really," one of the knights said, "Fia...thanks. Your orders were super easy to follow in that fight against the flower-horned deer, even if you did lie about having experience."

"For sure! Captain Cyril sure hammered down on us for not knowing about the monster though. But, like, how were we supposed to remember a monster we'd pretty much never encounter? Sure, it was in our jurisdiction, and we did get a monster list, but I haven't looked at that thing in years! No way I'd remember!"

"Totally. We'd be deer dinner if it weren't for you, Fia. Thanks a bunch. And now...let's drink! And then eat some more!"

One of the knights slapped my back and said, "Hey, Fia! You might be a newbie, but you're already one of us, ya hear? So no more of that formal talk with us, okay?"

"Yes, sir! From this point onward, Fia Ruud shall speak freely!"

"Ain't nothing 'freely' about that!" the three rebutted before breaking into laughter.

And then...we drank! We drank, uh...drinks. There were *lots*. The Unit Three knights kept refilling my glass over and over and, giddy as I was, I downed every one they poured until I'd totally lost track of time—

Hm? Who's that?

There was a topless man beside me, talking vigorously about... something.

Huh? Who was this guy again? I felt like I'd seen him before... Oh, wait! He was that guy standing behind Cyril earlier.

"And so—hey, you listening, Fia?!" bellowed the man with auburn-colored hair, who was...uh. Loud? And I definitely remembered him, kinda.

"Huh? Uh, my apologies. Could you repeat yourself?" But the Unit Three knights were looking over at me sheepishly for some reason...?

Oh, right... I promised to stop speaking so politely.

"Er...so, what's up with the no shirt?" I asked, speaking freely. The Unit Three knights immediately seemed flustered, which I thought was odd. They were the ones who told me to stop speaking casually in the first place!

"I said the captain has a six-pack!" the man yelled.

"Six...pack?" I mumbled. Pack of...what? Wait, was he talking about face packs? I know a lot of ladies use those to moisturize their skin and such, but I couldn't imagine Saviz sticking six of them on his face at once. "Captain's face isn't *that* big...is it?"

"What are you talking about? Where did faces come into this? Are you even listening?!"

"Um, *yeah*? And *you* just said that the captain sticks on six face packs, *pfft*! Brutal," I slurred.

"What are you talking about?!" he exclaimed. "I'm just saying that the captain's abdominal muscles are split into six sections!"

"Abdominal muscles? *Abdominal?* That sounds pretty risqué! Can you just say that kind of thing?!"

"W-wait, can I?!" the auburn-haired man wondered. "Sh-shoot, are the military police gonna arrest me? Y-you guys, go fill Desmond's cup until he's too plastered to do anything!"

His subordinates got to work, and auburn-head got back to talking. "Listen up, Fia," he said, pointing at his bare chest, "you see these abs of mine?! How many do you see!"

"Umm...one, two, three...four! We're lookin' at four, chief!"

"That's right, four abs! And since the number of abs you have is determined at birth, I'll *always* have four abs no matter how many years I train or how many monsters I kill!" And at that, the auburn-haired man began to weep uncontrollably.

"Ah...there he goes again," said a Unit Three knight wearily.

"Already back to the usual drunken grumbling," said another with a sigh.

Then another knight called out to me. "Sorry about that, Fia," he said with a sympathetic sigh. "Captain Zackary always gets like this after a few drinks. He finds a drinking partner and complains about the same thing every time. We're all tired of it, but there's not much we can do."

"Hate to say it, but you're the sacrifice for the day. We've all put up with him again and again, so can you take the hit this time?"

Sounds like everybody's got it rough, I thought drunkenly. *But what's wrong with having a four-pack? Umm...okay, what's this knight's name again? Flannery? No, Zackary?*

"Look at me, Zackary!" I said, proudly unbuttoning the top of my knight uniform.

"F-Fia, what the hell are you doing?!" he said, flustered.

I looked at Zackary defiantly as I stripped and tossed my top away. "Behold!" The undershirt I wore underneath my uniform outlined my stomach clearly. "A *four*-pack? I have a *one*-pack! Every day I train and train, but I can't gain a single muscle!" I proudly thrust out my bulging stomach. From the corner of my eye I saw Cyril, who'd been watching me from a distance away, spit out his drink.

"Wh-wh-what the hell..." Zackary stammered.

"The audacity, complaining about having a four-pack when so many of us struggle with having a one-pack in this cruel world! Or...or, no! Maybe I should just call this a *no*-pack!" I paused. "'Cause I got no muscle," I added, for clarity's sake.

"F-Fia..." Zackary stammered, looking down at my tummy disapprovingly. "I think you've let yourself go too much. A chubby stomach is cute when it's on a child like my three-year-old niece, but for an adult..."

"Oh, *thanks*! I'll get right on it. Oh, wait—turns out I've trained every single day for my entire life because I wanted to be a knight. Whoops! *Every. Single. Day!* Even after becoming a knight, I *still* haven't missed a day of training! And what do I have to show for it? At the end of it all, I'm still stuck with this tummy! Tell me, *Zack*. What ex-*Zack*-tly am I supposed to do?!"

Okay, okay, it wasn't nearly as dire as I was pretending. My stomach was just a little bloated because I'd been eating and drinking at the festival. But Zackary didn't need to know that.

Zackary's eyes floated back and forth between my face and stomach. Eventually, he groaned and, with a bitter expression, said, "Fia...at this point, I suggest you just give up on ever gaining muscle. And...you probably shouldn't show that stomach to anyone again if you can. Or even talk about it at all."

"What?!" I glared at him, burning with indignation. "You. *You.* You come at me *bragging* about your four-pack and you say *that*?! Who do you think you are, you big, hypocritical little...Zack?!"

"N-no, I was just thinking for your *own* sake, you see, I—"

"Oh, for *my* sake! Wow, thanks! What, do you wanna trade? I'll take your four pack and you get this tummy of mine!"

"*Nooo!*" he screamed. "I-I mean, um. That's a little much..."

I jabbed a finger at him. "Then don't *ever* brag about your four-pack again! It's disrespectful to me! I have nothing, you hear me?! I lack the packs!"

"F-forgive me! I swear, I'll never talk about abs again." As Zackary slumped to his knees and made his promise, the onlooking Six Knight Brigade knights erupted into cheers.

"Holy crap, Fia! You're incredible!"

"We've been saved from the captain's endless cycle of complaining!"

True to his word, Zackary never spoke of abdominal muscles again, but...I would later come to be known as the "Chubby Savior" among the Sixth Knight Brig—wait, really? Oh, come on!

15
A Chat with the Brigades' Top Three

AFTER ZACKARY promised to never talk about abdominal muscles again, Cyril came over and took me away. He seemed pretty miserable, muttering something about "acting your age" and "lack of femininity."

After passing through numerous long, winding hallways, we arrived in a room far more regal than the rest.

Where are we? The room was ridiculously spacious, lined with soft carpet and furnished with stately bookshelves, with a work desk wedged unobtrusively into the mix.

The ceiling was surprisingly tall. I stared up at it; paintings of the knight brigades and saints stared back.

"Over here, Fia." Saviz and Desmond were sitting on sofas next to a low table in a corner of the room.

"Good evening, Captain Saviz, Captain Desmond." I greeted them politely before breaking into a devious grin. "Ueh heh heh. Hey, Captain Desmond? I've found some top-secret info you might want to hear."

"Oh? Go on, then. We'll see if it's as secret as you say." Desmond gave me a thoughtful, curious sort of look—obviously. He was commandant of the military police, after all, so of course he'd be interested in any new secret information.

I, Fia Ruud, was more than happy to provide such important data! "The secret info is...risqué personal information about the captain!"

Desmond blinked. "What?"

"Captain Saviz has a six-pack! *Ta-da!* Can you believe it?!"

"Is...that all? I'm fairly certain that everyone in the knight brigades already knows...that."

"*Whaaat?!* It's a leak! An information leak! Isn't that a problem?!" I cried frantically.

Cyril, right behind me, let out a sigh. "I apologize. To speak frankly, the girl is wasted."

"Eh heh heh, meeee? I'm just tipsy! Look, I'm *fine*! I can keep it up! And I haven't forgotten about that good, good alcohol the captain promised me."

"That's nice to hear. Why don't you come sit down, then?" Saviz granted us permission to sit and briefly glanced toward the door. A servant appeared with new glasses and poured us a golden-colored drink. "It's noble rot wine. It's sweet, so it should suit your taste."

"It's...noble rot wine?!" I held up my glass reverently. "So expensive, so delicious... Is it really okay for me to drink it?!"

"Indeed it is," said Saviz. "You fought well today. This celebration is for you. Glory to the Náv Black Dragon Knights."

"Glory to the Náv Black Dragon Knights!" Cyril, Desmond, and I echoed, then moved our glasses to our lips.

Ah...delicious. The noble rot is super sweet—Saviz chose well. It's leagues better than the wine at the meat festival, I...think. I don't know. I'm no wine connoisseur.

"Thank you for saving me today, Captain," I said with a smile. At the end of it all, the one who contributed the most to slaying the flower-horned deer was him—and with a single swing no less. Which reminded me... "S-sir, did you get a chance to eat the flower-horned deer meat yet?! I didn't think, but—I—you—you've earned that meat the most! Oh no...why was I so entranced by my own piece of meat! I could have secured your piece too! M-maybe there's still some left?"

I stood up to go grab some meat when Saviz raised his hand to stop me. "I don't need a child worrying about me. Sit down." It was then I noticed the huge spread of fruit, cheese, and ham on the table.

I sat back down on the sofa. *Oh, I guess he's good for snacks. Oops.*

"You're a strange one," he continued. "You're able to fight a monster you've never seen before with information alone. You can determine health by sight. Even a monster's unique traits are known to you in a flash." Saviz sipped his wine before continuing. "I think your eyes are something special."

"My eyes? Um, I guess my eyesight's pretty good?"

"Be quiet, Fia," Cyril chided, "before you say something stupid again!"

S-sorry! I thought I was supposed to respond!

I figured Saviz was pausing to think again, but it seemed he was just handing the baton over to Desmond.

He began to speak now, swirling the contents of his glass as he grasped it by the bowl with all five fingers. "You know, I just can't get a read on what you really are. You're always showing everyone up, but it doesn't look like you have some special ability. As far as I can tell, you aren't *lying* about anything, hmm? You've done the impossible many times over but fail to even recognize how impressive your own accomplishments are... It's enough to make me wonder what the hell I've been working so hard for. You're going to leave my pride in shambles, you know."

Um, Cyril told me to be quiet, but does that still apply? Desmond just complimented me (maybe), so shouldn't I thank him? Or maybe I should compliment him back? He seems a bit down...

I looked over at Cyril, who dryly shook his head. Keep quiet, then.

With nothing to talk about, the four of us drank in silence. I had to wonder, were elites always like this? The silence made me feel—what's the word—meditative? My eyelids started to feel heavy and...and...

Zzz...

My pillow...moved? That couldn't be right.

I opened my eyes to find my head on Cyril's lap.

A lap pillow...ha ha! I used Cyril's lap as a pillow! He's...oh no, he's gonna kill me!

I shot up in a panic. "I'm sorry, Captain! I was just doing

some extended meditation!" As I sat up, someone's uniform top slipped off of me. I looked at Cyril to see...he only had a shirt on?! "Nngh! I even took away your uniform?! Forgive me!"

"I gave it to you myself. And I'm not so cruel that I'd get mad over something like this," Cyril laughed, and even his laughs dripped with elegance. "You slept pretty well. This is the first time I've seen anyone fall asleep in the captain's—no, the King's younger brother's own room."

"*Eeek!* The captain's room? And he's royalty too?! No wonder it's so fancy!"

Saviz gave a mild shrug from across the table. "Children need their sleep."

As for Desmond, he was beside him, still drinking his wine. That meant I hadn't been "meditating" for all *that* long, thank goodness. I forced a smile. "Ha ha, I *was* meditating, you know. Because of how safe I felt? With the strongest knight by my side? Yep!"

Everyone stiffened immediately, but I didn't notice. I was too busy wondering whether I should ask for another glass of noble rot wine.

"Fia?" asked Cyril gently. "Who do you mean by 'strongest knight'?"

What's with him? Fishing for compliments?

"You, of course. I've seen you all swing your swords by now, and I can tell Captain Cyril's attack and speed are the highest. You seem to have a bad habit of holding back when doing combat, but in a contest of pure strength, you'd take first! Don't you think so?"

Cyril's expression clouded over. Uh. Oops?

"Your eyes still continue to amaze me..." said Cyril. "I thought it was odd that you were slow to recognize the captain's presence earlier today with the flower-horned deer, but I never would have thought you'd discover *this*."

"Ah, th-that, forgive me! The moment Captain Cyril arrived, I figured we had enough strength present to defeat the monster and so I turned my attention back toward it! And, um...by the way, I, uh, I also couldn't help noticing that the monster recognized you as the strongest person there too. That's why it barreled towards you, which gave the captain a clear shot at it. Of course, I'm sure you stood next to him knowing that would happen."

"I...understand now," said Cyril. "Your ability to grasp the battlefield is perfect. I'm sorry for looking down on you until now."

"Huh? *Huh*?! Wh-wh-wh-wh-wh-*what*, no! I'm the one who's sorry for talking out of turn!"

Did Cyril just apologize to me? But I'm...I'm the one always apologizing to him, right?!

"I have something to ask of you, Fia," he began, wearing a thin smile. "Can you keep the fact that I'm stronger than the captain a secret? It's easier for the knights to follow the captain if they think he's the strongest. For similar reasons, I'd prefer not to stand out."

I nodded furiously. *O-of course I'll keep it a secret! I wouldn't dream of inconveniencing him!*

I was still bobbing my head up and down when Saviz broke his silence. "Fia...could you go to the Fourth Monster Tamer Knight Brigade?"

"Huh?" I answered blankly, surprised by the sudden request.

Why there? And why do I suddenly feel like I'm forgetting somebody important...

A Tale of the
Secret
Saint

16
What It Means to Be a Saint

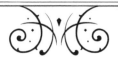

SEEING MY CONFUSION, Cyril explained what Saviz meant about me going to the Fourth Monster Tamer Knight Brigade. "You can determine the health of monsters, and he wants to make use of that ability. The knights of the Fourth Monster Tamer Knight Brigade all have at least one familiar, but they only have a rough estimate of how much health their familiars have. If they knew, they could use that knowledge in battle."

"I-I see...but more than half of what I do is just intuition and assumption..." I could confidently determine health give or take ten units, but calculating the exact number was all guesswork. I was less competent than they knew...

He nodded at my words and gave me a small smile. "It won't be an official transfer. That would cause problems when we need to move you back to the First Knight Brigade, so we're planning to make it a temporary assignment."

H-huh? Problems? I won't cause any problems if they transfer me...!

Cyril continued, "You're the cute little mascot of the First Knight Brigade, after all. I don't intend to give you away so easily. I get the feeling the captain of the Fourth Monster Tamer Knight Brigade won't want to give you up either, once he figures out your worth. That's why we won't transfer you officially. That being said, if you get mistreated or otherwise are inconvenienced by all of this, please let me know immediately, okay?"

Who was he calling a cute little mascot?! Nope, I'd just let that one slide. I was a mature adult, after all. "Um, okay. Just wondering, but if something like that did occur and I told you, what would happen?"

"Ha ha! Well, the person or people in question would be gone the next day...and *no one* would dare make the same mistake again." He smiled gently, and I felt shivers run down my spine. Yeah, my intuition said that I probably shouldn't tell him about any problems I had unless I absolutely needed to.

"Goodness, it's already so late," said Cyril. "Shall we retire for the night?" While Desmond and I were preparing to leave, Saviz mentioned that he had business at the knight dormitories to take care of. In the end, all four of us headed there together.

The night sky held a beautiful moon, and the wind blew gently, bringing with it the scents of the night.

Still drunk, I walked forward vacant-minded when Saviz broke the silence. "I understand that today was the first time you've fought alongside the saints, Fia. Any impressions?"

"They're horrible," I said, then realized my rudeness and added, "...Sir."

Cyril froze at my remark and Desmond seemed to scowl... but Saviz's expression didn't fluctuate one bit. "The saints?" he asked.

"No," I said, "the ones who twisted what it means to be a saint. What I saw today wasn't right at all! I think...if the Great Saint from three hundred years ago could see what they'd become, she'd be devastated."

Who...who am I kidding? She did see...and she cried.

"Maybe she'd even cry," I said aloud.

"Do you think so? Is that something else you learned through books?" Saviz asked, quieter this time.

"No. Just my personal opinion. Hey, Captain...how do you feel about the saints? Do you want to worship them like gods too? Heh heh, no...of course not. Saints aren't a bunch of distant, fickle gods. No, the saints are the shield of the knights..."

I looked up at the sky, and the moon wobbled. My balance was *wayyy* off. *Mm-hmm...yeah, I'm drunk.* "But that's all just my opinion," I added. "Don't forget, you're the one who asked."

On a whim, I slipped off my boots and held them in my hand as I tottered forward. Just wanted to go barefoot, I guess. But nobody said a word of complaint about it; we walked the rest of the way in silence.

I woke up the next morning with a splitting headache.

Ugh, head! Stop throbbing! It's like somebody is tap dancing on my head—tap, tap, tap, tap—ack, go away! I feel like I'm gonna puke. Water...I need water. What even is this?

"Looks like a hangover."

I looked up to find my roommate Olga standing there.

"A hangover? That sounds pretty adult, right?"

"Like hell it does." Despite her harsh words, she handed me a glass of water.

I glugged the whole thing down in a snap. "Delicious!" I stood up, feeling refreshed.

"Huh? You're already better?"

"Heh heh! That's youth for ya, Olga."

"I don't care how old you are, *nobody* gets over a hangover with just one glass of water!"

Wait, what was that smell? I sniffed myself, and *ugh*. I reeked of alcohol. Nope, I wasn't going to spend the morning like *that*. Totally improper! I took a towel and headed for the shower.

"Adulthood stinks," I said to Olga. "I'm gonna go wash it off real quick."

After a refreshing shower, I went to the training grounds for some sword practice.

No sooner had I arrived when Fabian called out to me, surprised. "Huh? Fia? I thought you were assisting the Fourth Monster Tamer Knight Brigade starting today."

"Huh? The Fourth Monster Tamer Knight Brigade?"

"Didn't you know? Captain Cyril just told me this morning."

Ah...I see. I bet he told me too. That...doesn't mean I remember.
I forced a smile. "I'm...gonna go see the captain."

"Come in." Cyril's voice called out from his office at the sound of my knock. I opened the door slowly to find him sitting at an office desk, looking exhausted.

"Oh? You seem tired for once."

"Fia...what is it?" he said in an oddly weary voice.

He must be overworked. "Um, well...I heard I was being transferred to the Fourth Monster Tamer Knight Brigade? So I came by to check..."

"Why? Didn't I say I'd transfer you just yesterday?"

We talked? Uh oh. I should choose my next words carefully...

"Forgive me, I misspoke. I am going to assist the Fourth Monster Tamer Knight Brigade, as we talked about together last night. Which both of us definitely know. So, you know, I just came here just in case you wanted me to relay something to them."

Cyril smiled icily. "You didn't happen to forgot my orders from yesterday, did you?" He was sharp, as was to be expected of the captain of the most prestigious brigade.

I maintained my smile, too afraid to give a solid yes or no.

His smile turned into a glare as he grew sure of his suspicions. "Tell me everything you remember of last night."

"Yes, sir. Partway through the meat festival, you called some of us over to lecture us. The flower-horned meat was delicious...and that's pretty much it?"

"That's basically nothing! Did you really forget everything in your drunken stupor?!"

"Forgive me!" It was exactly as he said—I had an ultra-powerful skill that erased memories whenever alcohol entered my system. While that meant I could forget all the embarrassing things I did when drunk...it could also be a pretty big inconvenience for everybody else! I lowered my head, sorry from the depths of my heart.

Cyril let out a deep sigh and flashed a defeated smile. "No, it's my fault for bringing up work at a celebration. I should be apologizing. Now, starting today, you will be assisting the Fourth Monster Tamer Knight Brigade by tracking the health of the Knights' familiars. Please note, though, that the knights in the Fourth Monster Tamer Knight Brigade tend to look down on those without familiars. If they treat you badly, please let me know."

"Um...okay."

"Oh, and another thing," he said, beckoning me closer. "Show me your wrists, just in case."

Huh? Does he want to check my injury from yesterday? Heh, I healed that up without a trace a long time ago! I extended my arms in front of him, perhaps a bit smugly.

His eyes widened. "A proof of pact... Fia, you have a familiar?"

A black ring, one millimeter thick, was still wrapped around my left wrist. *Oh, of course. He was checking for a familiar pact. Why, yes indeed, sir! I have a pact with a legendary-class monster, a black dragon!*

I...couldn't really say that, right?

A Tale of the
Secret
Saint

17

The Fourth Monster Tamer Knight Brigade Part 1

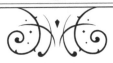

I STARED AT CYRIL.

Should I even tell him about my black dragon familiar? He traced the black ring around my left wrist with his finger thoughtfully. "It's fine," he said finally. "You don't need to tell me what kind of monster it is; you're not required to report familiar pacts made before entering the brigades. But if, by some one-in-a-million-chance, you *did* have a powerful familiar, you might be pressured into transferring to the Fourth Monster Tamer Knight Brigade."

"If any of the knights ask you about it," he added with a quick pat on my head, "just keep quiet and smile. The knights of the Monster Tamer Knight Brigade tend to judge others by the strength of their familiars, and they'll probably look down on you for having a weak one. It's better to just keep quiet and leave them guessing."

"Uh...what makes you think my familiar is weak?"

He chuckled lightly, a smile appearing on his face. "Ah ha ha, oh dear. It's precisely because you ask those sorts of questions.

You clearly don't know much about familiars, and so I suspect that yours is weak. You see, the width of the mark on one's arm is an indication of the strength of a familiar. The thicker the line, the stronger the monster. The weakest monsters, H-rank, have a width of about one centimeter."

Huh? Wait, Zavilia's weak? But...he seemed so strong when we met! Explain yourself, Zavilia!

"Though the *reason* for the different widths is interesting. You see, the mark is actually an indicator of how long it took to make the monster submit to the pact. If the knight is far stronger than the monster, or if the monster was willing, it's conceivable that the pact line could be deceptively thin."

Oh. That makes sense. I mean, Zavilia did kill a bunch of A-rank monsters while I slept. Yeah, no way could he be weak! Heh...I mean, obviously! I never doubted you, buddy!

"Putting that aside," he said, "you should just smile and bluff about the strength of your monster. And I recommend not mentioning what kind of monster you have, either. That being said, I've never seen a proof of pact only a millimeter thick before. No, you probably won't fool anyone." Cyril put his fingers to his chin, deep in thought. "It may be obvious that you just found some injured H-rank monster and instantly made a pact with it, but... hmm..."

His mumbling petered out at the end, but I got the gist.

Don't worry, Captain! I understand what you mean completely! Showing them my dragon isn't going to help. No, I'll be better off making them think I have a familiar even more powerful than a dragon! Don't worry, your brilliant and discerning subordinate knows exactly what you mean to say! I gave Cyril a knowing smile. Yeah, we were definitely on the same page.

He replied with a long, tired sigh.

Wow...he must be really burned out from work. "You seem more exhausted than usual, Captain. Have you considered taking a break?" I said as considerately as I could.

He narrowed his eyes. "You...really don't remember anything from yesterday, do you? Yesterday, a certain someone told me I was horrible directly to my face. I'm still reeling a bit."

"Th-they said what?! T-to you?! Who is this fool?! Wait, were they killed on the spot?!"

"No," he sighed, his eyes still narrowed on me. "In fact, they seem to be in rather good spirits."

Jeez, he seems really out of it. Well...as his subordinate, I have a duty to cheer him up! "You don't need to worry about some jerk like that! Any real decent knight would never say something so crass. I can't even imagine it!"

"Really," he said in a deadpan voice. "*You* can't even imagine it?"

H-huh? What a weird reaction. "Y-yeah? Th-they'd have to be either stupidly brave or suicidal to say something so reckless to you."

"To me? Ah, but it was directed at the captain too."

"Th-the captain?! I-Isn't that treason?! They'd get the death penalty—no, the knights would beat them to death before the trial!"

What kind of madman would say that? They'd have to be nuts! Just the thought alone sends shivers down my spine.

But Cyril shook his head. "They weren't in trouble at all. You see, they were just a child. As a matter of fact, it was an answer to the captain's own question."

"Ohh, a child! Well, that makes sense. I'm sure they apologized?"

"Surprisingly, no. In fact, it seems they've already forgotten the whole debacle. The ones who are *really* in trouble are the ones stuck taking care of that child," he said wearily.

Hmm? I wonder what that's about.

"Anyway, Fia...you've learned that I'm stronger than the captain, yes? Well, you agreed yesterday to do your best to keep that a secret. Could you give me your word once again?"

"Yes, sir! I would never do anything to inconvenience you! You have my word!" My eyes twinkled.

He took his deepest sigh yet. "Perhaps our definition of 'inconvenience' differs..."

As I walked down the long hall to the Fourth Monster Tamer Knight Brigade, I began thinking to myself, *I have to nail this first impression. Maybe...I should bring a gift? Wait, no, it's too late for that. What to do...*

Before I knew it, I was at the Monster Tamer Brigade captain's door. I knocked. "Excuse me! I'm Fia Ruud from the First Knight Brigade! Um, pardon me!"

I entered the room and found a single knight crudely sprawled out on a chair. His brow wrinkled as he shouted, "Sure took your sweet time, didn't you? I was told you'd arrive first thing in the morning! Or is this what counts as 'first thing in the morning' to the First Knight Brigade?"

Ack—botched it already! "I'm sorry I'm late!" I said, bowing my head.

The knight stood up, nearly knocking his chair over. "I'm Gideon Oakes, vice-captain of the Fourth Monster Tamer Knight Brigade. Our captain is away for the time being, so I'm in charge."

He looked like he was in his mid-thirties. He was a large man, and arrogance positively *dripped* from every pore. He tousled his short, reddish-brown hair and turned up his nose. "Great... another useless one. So Captain Cyril really recommended some brat, hm?"

Oof...he seems unhappy. Maybe he's not a morning person?

"Why were you assigned here anyway?" he drawled. "Does the First Knight Brigade truly respect us so little? Shuffling their knights off to us just because they're supposed to be the *best.* Hmph. Nothing but trouble for the rest of us!"

Yeaaaah, I have to agree. I mean, the guy only got these orders a day in advance. Cyril's a slave driver for sure...

"So, what?" Gideon asked. "You're going to measure the health of our monsters? Oh, thank you *ever* so much, how would we survive without you?" He wiggled his arms in mock helplessness before slamming them down on the table with a scowl. "Ha! Get real, brat!"

What a...colorful guy. Not a bad person, probably, but what was I even supposed to say to that?

Fortunately, there was a knock on the door before I had to answer.

"Come in!" Gideon said, and a woman with bright-green hair in her mid-twenties stepped in.

Ooh, she's pretty!

"I'm sorry to interrupt your conversation, Vice-Captain, but you have a call from R."

"What?! I'll be there right away!" He bolted for the door and paused, suddenly seeming to remember me. "I've no orders for you. Just kill time somewhere." And he was gone.

It was just me and the bright-green haired woman in the room now. I spoke first. "Nice to meet you. I'm Fia Ruud, from the First Knight Brigade."

"Nice to meet you, Fia. The name's Patty Conaghan. I'm part of the Fourth Monster Tamer Knight Brigade, and I'm the vice-captain's assistant."

"Oh! So...you must also give orders, then? Because the vice-captain made it sound like there was nothing for me to do, but it'd be great if I had an assignment!"

"Hee hee...goodness, Captain Cyril did send a young one, eh? I'm sorry about Vice-Captain Gideon's attitude. He has it out for the First Knight Brigade a bit. Thinks we're not treated as equal to the other brigades."

What, so he was just lashing out?

"He can be a little childish at times," she continued, "but he's no fool. He takes his work seriously. I'm sure he'll calm down and give you something to do soon enough. Until then, do you mind waiting here?"

Yeah...Patty seems to respect him, so I guess I was right. He doesn't seem like a bad person at all. "Of course—I'll just wait here. But, um, who's this 'R' person? Vice-Captain Gideon seemed in a hurry... Does he, uh, have a lover?"

"Ha ha ha, him? A lover?! No way! 'R' is the monster he has a pact with."

"Ohh."

"Familiars don't like it when somebody other than their master calls them by name. We call them by their first initial instead," she said. "Why don't we sit down?"

She directed me to a sofa in the corner of the room and started preparing some tea. Then she pulled out a yellow tin with cookies from a nearby cupboard and arranged them for me on a plate. "Despite how he looks, the vice-captain's got quite a sweet tooth."

Oh really? Him, of all people? He seemed like the kind of guy to eat nothing but meat for every meal.

"Seeing as this is your first time here, let me tell you a little about our duty. The Fourth Monster Tamer Knight Brigade specializes in making pacts with monsters and putting those monsters to good use. Making the pact is the most difficult part, but caring for them after that still keeps us busy. Some monsters can be quite finicky and spoiled, but meeting their needs is important. If you give them what they need, they'll reward you with obedience."

Wait...really? But I haven't seen Zavilia once since the day we made a pact. Am I doing it wrong? "They won't attack you if you neglect them, will they?" I asked, worriedly.

"They won't *attack*, per se, but they might pout and body slam you. Perhaps whip you with their tail too, if they have one. It's quite a problem with the larger monsters."

Wait... Zavilia's a larger monster! And he has a tail! I'm dead! I'm dragon-dinner-dead!

"Is something the matter?" she said, noticing my silence.

"No, well, uh...actually? I made a pact with a monster a while ago, and I've kind of neglected it since. Do you think it'll be mad at me?"

"Really?! Show me your arm!" She grabbed my arm and pulled up my sleeve before I could even respond. She looked disappointed when she saw the skinny mark on my left wrist.

"Ah." With that, her curiosity seemed satisfied. "Well...it's impressive enough for a knight outside the Fourth Monster Tamer Knight Brigade to make a pact. The vice-captain will be a while. You should take this chance to go meet with your familiar if they're in the woods nearby."

"Wait, really?" I bounded off the sofa and gave Patty a quick bow. "I'll be off then!"

"Uh. Just like that? I...don't think you should go into the woods alone. At least join up with the Sixth Knight Brigade on an expedition."

"I'll be fine! I'll stay by the entrance, not go in!"

"I suppose that makes sense, yes. Your familiar would have to be on the very outskirts of the woods. That mark is so thin, after all..." Was I good? It looked like I was good, so I bolted out the door.

Now I was worried about Zavilia. He was strong enough to beat a bunch of A-rank monsters, but he still had a lot of injuries when we first met. What if he was getting bullied by even stronger monsters?

What'll I do if he's injured again? I thought as I spurred my horse toward the nearest forest. Zavilia told me the pact would allow him to hear my call from anywhere—but I wasn't about to call a dragon to a castle or a city, so the forest was the smart option.

I got off my horse and immediately began shouting. "Zavilia! Zavilia!" My voice echoed through the silent forest.

In an instant, the sky opened as if slashed by an impossibly massive blade. The line stretched into an ellipse, and within it raged dark clouds, rain, and thunder—scenery from somewhere *else*. And from the chaos descended a black dragon, its wings spread wide. The creature was far more beautiful than anything I'd ever seen, ten meters tall with individual scales that shone like they'd been chiseled by a master artist. I never realized that there were so many shades of black.

Long ago, I'd heard that dragons were the first and most complete beings in existence. Right at that moment, I truly understood what that meant.

I couldn't help but stare in amazement as it spread its elegant wings and swooped downward. *But wait...isn't Zavilia supposed to be much smaller than this? His scales weren't this shiny, either.*

Umm...pardon me, but who might you be?

"Fia! You called for me!" The black dragon spoke cheerily despite my confusion.

"Um, you're...Zavilia?" That clear, high-pitched voice sounded right, at least.

"Did you forget about me already?" he said, hanging his massive, beautiful head sadly.

"N-no, of course not!" I said as I stroked his scales. "I just didn't recognize you. You've grown a lot—your wings and body are bigger, and your scales are all sparkly. You look nothing like you did four months ago."

"Hee hee, that's 'cause I'm in my growth period!"

"Really? Wait, how old are you?"

"Zero."

"Z-zero?!"

You're a baby, then! Dragons lived long lives, so I assumed he was older. I guess I assumed wrong. "A-aw, li'l Zavvy babyboo! Mama Fia will take care of you, okay? Are you hungywungy?"

"Ha ha! Dragons and humans age differently. In your human life span, I'm the equivalent of twelve or thirteen. In only another half a year, I shall be an adult."

"O-oh. Wait—you're going to get even bigger?"

"Indeed. Perhaps twice my current size?"

Whoa. The idea alone made my head spin. And here I'd been worrying about other monsters bullying him, wondering if I should bring him home, but...at *this* size? Where would he even go? He definitely couldn't fit in my room now...

Zavilia looked at me curiously. **"Is something the matter? Can I help?"**

"I was thinking of taking you back with me if you wanted, but you're a lot bigger than I thought you'd be..."

"Oh? Can I really come with you?" His blue eyes gleamed.

"Yeah, but I don't have a place where you could stay at your size."

"Easily solved!" he said. In an instant, he rapidly shrank down until he was small enough to sit on my two open palms.

"Z-Z-Z-Z-Zavilia?! Wh-what are you doing? I-isn't this bad for your growth?"

"No, it won't be a problem. I'm simply shrinking. The way I returned to infancy when I was injured was a completely different ability—no need for concern."

"I-is that right..." I didn't really understand the difference, but I thought it best to just move things along. I was more concerned about something else. "Zavilia, can you change your color? The only black-winged monsters are black dragons. Even if you're tiny, it's pretty obvious what you are."

The little dragon looked down sadly. **"My apologies, Fia, but I take a lot of pride in my color. I will not change it."**

"I see...hee hee! That's all right, I just thought of something! Can you hunt down a winged monster for me?"

"Easily, but, well...your 'good ideas' tend to have questionable results," he said, returning to his original size. **"Can you cover your ears for a moment?"** I put my hands over my ears, and he opened his mouth and let out an enormous roar. **"Graoooooooooooh!"**

The ground shook and the air trembled. Leaves rustled throughout the forest. Faraway objects came crashing to the ground.

"Oh right," the dragon mused. **"I suppose there aren't many monsters this close to the edge of the forest. I'll go collect a few."** With a flap of his huge wings, he left me behind. I stood there, dazed by what just happened.

Those crashing noises...d-d-d-did he just kill monsters with his roar alone? My legs gave out, and suddenly I was sitting on the earth. *That seems...bad?! Zavilia's way stronger than I thought. He's nothing like he was before.*

When I introduced Zavilia to my family as a familiar, I narrowly avoided trouble—but now? No way. I had no idea how strong the other knights' familiars were, but they couldn't be close to this. Maybe I could make it work? Maybe?

Zavilia came back soon enough with a dozen or so monsters in his jaw. I took two bluebird-type monsters from among them and put them in my bag.

"Do you want to come back with me now?" I asked. "I don't mind coming back another time if there's someone you need to say bye to."

He hung his head. **"That's all right. I've been alone long enough..."**

"O-oh, right. Um, can you shrink down now?" I said, un-buttoning the top of my knight uniform. I placed Zavilia, now smaller, inside my uniform, and buttoned it back up just enough to hold him in place.

"It's not too tight, is it? Just hang in there until we get back."

"You're warm..."

He stopped moving soon after, and I wondered if he fell asleep. *Yep, little kids sure fall asleep fast!* They said that children who slept more grew more—I hoped Zavilia would grow up nice and healthy.

I got on my horse and tried to ride back as smoothly as I could. When I reached the Royal Castle, I immediately made for the Fourth Monster Tamer Knight Brigade. But first, I happened across some knights of the Sixth Knight Brigade.

"F-Fia? Um, what's with the gut?"

"Wow...you might want to cut back on the snacks a bit."

Huh? They couldn't really *think this is my gut, right?! What's with these Sixth Knight Brigade guys, always so rude about my appearance?*

A little miffed, I made my way to the Fourth Monster Tamer Knight Brigade building and came across Gideon. The moment he spotted me, he put his hands on his waist and his face twisted back into a scowl. "If it isn't Little Miss 'I got a recommendation from the First Knight Brigade's captain'. Takin' a stroll, are we?"

"No, I just got back from some business in the forest."

"Hmph!" He started to walk past me in a huff. Then, as if suddenly remembering something, he stopped to grab my arm. "Oh yeah, I heard you have a familiar. Let me see your arm."

Without waiting for my reply, he pushed my sleeves up. His assistant, Patty, had done the same. *Are all knights of the Fourth Monster Tamer Knight Brigade like this?*

Gideon looked at my left wrist and blinked a few times. He brought his face closer to it, staring. "Huh? Why's the mark so thin?" he muttered. "What kind of monster did you pact with?" He shot me a venomous glare. "Wow, lucky you," he said in a mocking tone. "You stumbled onto a half-dead monster to form a pact with."

"Huh?! How'd you know?!"

He scowled. "'Cause I'm a hundred times smarter than your pint-sized brain could ever even comprehend! You think you're hot stuff just 'cause you made a pact with some weak, runty monster? You could have a hundred pacts and you wouldn't be worth the crap on my boot!"

Huh? I thought Cyril said leaving them guessing would make them think my familiar was stronger than it was? But isn't Gideon completely underestimating me right now?

I tried thinking back to Cyril's words.

If I recall correctly, he said to...smile and bluff about how strong my monster is. Oh, and not to let them know what kind it really is! And that's what I've been doing!

I put on a haughty smile and looked up at him. "Oh dear, Vice-Captain Gideon...my familiar isn't some run-of-the-mill weakling. It's the strongest, most ancient...oops!" I put my hand to my mouth, pretending I'd almost let a secret slip. "I've already said too much!"

"Are you an idiot?" he snarled. "Just look at yourself—weak, small, thin—you're clearly the puniest, weakest knight in all of the brigades. So what's your game? You thought you'd be a tamer 'cause you couldn't cut it as a knight? I bet your familiar's just like you—runty, mouthy, and worthless."

His face was almost touching mine at this point, his eyes full of disdain. "You know," he continued, "there's bottom feeders like you everywhere. Flatterers and brownnosers. Did you lick Captain Cyril's shoes? 'Oh, please, let me go play in the Fourth Monster Tamer Knight Brigade!' Pfft! I bet you thought you were *so* smart, making a pact with a monster on the brink of death and getting moved to the Fourth Monster Tamer Knight Brigade. Deluding yourself into thinking you'd finally have some worth. You're the lowest of the low. Scum."

I blinked a few times. He'd rattled on a bit long. Maybe I'd lost the thread a little? Because...I mean...

Did I screw up somewhere? Vice-Captain Gideon was supposed to tremble in fear after imagining just how powerful my familiar might be, so why's he's so angry? Forgive me, Captain Cyril...I didn't mean to mess up your brilliant plan! I hung my head dejectedly.

At that moment, footsteps rang out from the end of the hall.

"Vice-Captain Gideon!" Patty called out hurriedly. "There's been a report that the Black King was spotted in Starfall Forest!"

"What?! Impossible!" Gideon roared, his scowl vanishing.

Starfall Forest? Wasn't that where I picked up Zavilia just now? I wonder what happened...

I watched them absently until Gideon noticed me.

"This is confidential," he bellowed. "So *scram*, kid!"

I nodded. "Pardon me, sir!"

Uhh...did he just dismiss me for the day? They don't seem to have any work for me to do, anyway. Whatever they're working on is confidential. Yeah, I guess I'll head back to the dorm.

It was still working hours, but he *did* tell me to scram. Besides, there was something I wanted to finish before my roommate Olga returned.

On the way back, I stopped by the canteen and got a bucket of hot water. I placed the two bird-type monster corpses Zavilia hunted in there. Zavilia was still sound asleep, so I left him in my uniform as I got to work. Once the hot water cooled off, I removed the monster corpses and plucked the feathers—they came out easily thanks to the hot water—all the while taking care not to create too big of a mess. Once I had enough feathers, I dumped the water and put the monster corpses in the empty bucket.

Great, now all I need to do is wash the feathers and then dry them. I don't need this monster meat. Maybe the canteen would want it?

I took a dry towel and wrapped the feathers, pressing on them to squeeze the water out. Once all the feathers were dried out, I took some blue fabric and started sewing the feathers in.

Zavilia didn't wake until the sun began to dip. Groggily, he muttered, **"I saw a dream of the past..."**

I couldn't help myself from laughing. "Oh, Zavilia, you silly goose. What past? You're zero years old!" I grinned broadly and brought out my new project from behind my back. "*Ta-da!* Your very own disguise!"

It was a miniature shirt with the feathers of a Blue Dove monster generously sewn into it. Zavilia was so happy at the sight that he was speechless!

When he finally spoke, he sounded overcome with emotion. **"Fia, don't tell me you want to disguise me as a Blue Dove..."**

"That's right, Zavilia! Such a smart little guy!"

He looked like he had something to say...but he chose to resign himself to his fate. Zavilia hopped into my lap and spread his wings. **"Do what you will."**

Carefully, I put the disguise on him. I'd made it so it could be tied under his chin and across his abdomen, with wings that slipped on. That way, none of the strings would show. Then I added the most important part—the beak.

I let out a sigh of satisfaction as I gazed at Zavilia's final form. "Perfect! I can't see any black on you at all! Everybody will think you're a Blue Dove!"

"A Blue Dove that's blind as a bat. How am I supposed to see in this?"

"Oh, I used two Blue Doves worth of feathers, so you're even fluffier than a normal one! Fancy, huh?"

"I'd rather have function over style when it comes to a disguise, but...thank you for making it fancy, Fia. I like it."

I stroked the blue wings of my new Blue Dove. "You know,"

I said dejectedly, "Captain Cyril actually gave me this really awesome plan, but I blew it. I wasn't supposed to show you off. Instead, everybody was going to be shaking in their boots, thinking I had some super powerful familiar."

"Oh? That's...uh, interesting."

"But I messed that up, so change of plans. Then again, I didn't really want people thinking I had some super scary powerful familiar anyway."

"Why not? The strength of your familiar determines your social status as a knight, yes? I suppose you wouldn't care much about that."

"Anyway!" I said, hugging Zavilia and then bringing him level with my eyes. "Now that you're here, we can work together! Of course, if you ever get bored, you can just nap in here or go play in the castle courtyard. But since you're so much stronger than I expected, we should probably hide that you're a black dragon for now, hence the disguise. Of course, if the other knights have familiars as strong as you, and if you don't want to make a bad impression, then I don't mind coming out and telling everybody about your black dragon-ness."

"I...don't see that happening. I'll be a Blue Dove for the time being, I suppose. Haah... I'm glad that I can be with you, Fia, but pretending to be the weakest monster is going to do a number on me," Zavilia grumbled. But at least he was happy to spend time with me, right?

Thank goodness I decided to bring him back. Now, next step!

"I'm going to practice bluffing like Captain Cyril wanted me to, okay?"

"Fia...don't. Just don't. This is not going to help anyone."

"Hee hee! Oh, Zavilia, you're still just a child. When you're older, you'll understand. Being an adult means putting thought into how you act."

"Oh, wow. You don't say. Well," he said defeatedly, "good luck." And with that, he closed his eyes.

Don't worry about a thing, Zavilia. I'll protect you. I won't let anyone pick on you ever again.

First thing the next morning, I went to the Fourth Monster Tamer Knight Brigade building. I noticed knights sneaking glimpses at my stomach as I walked by, but they couldn't think this was my actual belly...right?

I spotted Patty at the end of the hallway. "Hi, Patty!"

She stared at my stomach appalled as I trotted towards her. "Wh-what's with your belly? Did you eat too much or something?"

"I brought my familiar today! He's still sleeping, so I'm keeping him in my uniform."

"Ohh, I see. We actually have familiar stables outside; you should take a look when you have a moment. Normally, we'd have someone show you around the brigade on your first day, but we're currently working on something urgent. Everyone's pretty busy. Do you mind if we save the tour for another day?"

"Of course! Is it all right if I look around for work to do by myself in the meantime?" I replied cheerfully.

"That'll be fine."

The idea of utilizing monsters was a relatively new idea, one that didn't exist at all in my past life. Sure, I'd made a pact with Zavilia, but I didn't actually know what that entailed. Maybe I could figure it out as I explored the Fourth Monster Tamer Knight Brigade!

I bowed and started getting ready to leave when I noticed Gideon walking by. "Good morning, Vice-Captain Gideon!"

"What, you're still around?" He gave me a sour look. "I don't care how many times you pop in to greet me; I have no interest in working with useless suck-ups like you!"

Patty grimaced. "Sir, I don't believe that's appropriate to say."

He ignored her. "Oh right, I know *exactly* what you can do! There's a bunch of injured familiars in the familiar stables. Fetch some healing potions from the saints in the castle and feed them to the familiars every day, morning and afternoon!"

"Sir, you can't just—" Patty began.

"Shut it! Go tell whoever's currently in charge that somebody new's going to be handling the healing potions!"

Vice-Captain Gideon treats outsiders really harshly, I thought to myself as he prattled on and on. *But I bet once you get on his good side, he's nice!*

Zavilia must have been woken up by Gideon's loud voice. He stirred under my uniform and then popped his head out beneath my chin.

"Whoa, what the heck?!" Gideon took a step back, surprised by the monster suddenly popping out from underneath my clothes.

Oooh, I can introduce Zavilia! "Heh heh, this is my super-cute familiar!" I said with a smile.

From beneath his fluffy exterior, Zavilia's clear blue eyes narrowed in on Gideon.

"Wh-what? That's not...a Blue Dove...is it?" Gideon seemed alarmed as he met Zavilia's eyes.

I did it! My needlework was good enough. A perfect disguise! "That's right! He's a Blue Dove!"

"Lies! Blue Doves are smaller than that! And that thing's neck is way too long!"

"Huh? Neck? Oh, uh...that's because...of our fight! Before I could make him submit to a pact, we had a long and grueling fight. It's all my fault, you see. I...pulled his neck too much, and now it's stuck like this."

"More lies! The mark around your arm is far too thin; your pact should have been instant!"

"Huh? Oh, yeah, well...I, um, pulled his neck really fast?" I said sheepishly.

Gideon seemed to rack his brain as he stared Zavilia down, but it really was just the neck that was a bit long. Every other part looked perfectly Blue Dove-ish. *Heh, I'll call that a win for my needlework!*

"I suppose a worthless master could only create a pact with such a weird-looking familiar. Can that thing even fly with its misshapen body? It's already the weakest monster, but this? You might as well euthanize the thing."

"What are you talking about? Can't you see how cute it is? It *has* to be strong!"

"What are *you* talking about?! What does being cute have to do with strength?! It...it isn't even cute, the awful little thing!"

Impossible! It's so small and fluffy, it has *to be cute! Vice-Captain Gideon wouldn't know cuteness if it slapped him across the face!* I sighed. *I guess it's up to me to teach him what cuteness is. Good grief.*

"You...you're just trying to mess with me, aren't you? Yeah, I knew it! That stuff never slips past me! How can you be so arrogant when you have the weakest monster as your familiar?" Gideon prattled. "You brainless little dolt!"

Zavilia kept quiet up until now, but perhaps he was getting bored of the conversation. He nuzzled closer to me and opened his mouth, emitting a strange cry:

"Idi—ot, idi—ot."

Gideon furrowed his brow. "Huh? Did...your familiar just talk?"

"Idi—ot, idi—ot, hal—fwit." Zavilia was mimicking bird sounds in the cutest little voice I'd ever heard!

Oh jeez, Zavilia. You knew I couldn't talk back to my superior and came to my rescue. What a good boy!

I looked as meek as I could manage. "Oh, yes! See, his voice box got damaged when his neck was stretched out and now the sounds he makes are all screechy. I'm sorry if the noise hurts your ears..."

"Hal—fwit, hal—fwit, dun—derhead."

"No, no, no! It's obviously mocking me!" Gideon exclaimed.

"Ha ha, what? It's a Blue Dove. Blue Doves can't talk."

Gideon bit his lip and glared at Zavilia.

"Idi—ot, idi—ot, dun—derhead."

Tee hee. In moderation, Zavilia, in moderation, I thought as I stroked Zavilia's head.

"Very well, then. I'll leave healing the familiars to you, Fia Ruud. Now, if you'll excuse me." Gideon turned on his heels and left us.

Zavilia looked over my shoulder and said, "Hal—fwit, hal—fwit, half-wit times a hundred."

"Yoooour *daaaamn familiaaaaaar*!" Gideon bellowed from a ways behind me.

Tsk, tsk. To think this is enough to rile up a vice-captain. Well, I have better things to do...

I left the building, took a moment to find my bearings, and made my way towards the castle.

Umm, first I need to get some healing potions from the saints, right?

Saints generally stayed at a church if they were unmarried or had their own homes otherwise, but a good number were situated in the royal castle—or more accurately, in a detached villa right next to the castle. It made it easy to summon them in case of emergencies.

It took me a good thirty minutes to reach the villa on foot.

I walked the entire way while carrying Zavilia under my uniform, so I probably got a decent workout. Zavilia hadn't moved an inch, probably asleep again.

When I finally reached the villa, I showed the healing potion exchange slip I'd received from Patty to a butler at the entrance. The butler took a glance at my lapel pin, gave me a puzzled expression, and finally led me to a waiting room just past the entrance.

Yeah, I imagine it's not every day someone from the First Knight Brigade comes by to do grunt work for the Fourth Monster Tamer Knight Brigade.

I gazed out the window while waiting...and that's when I noticed the women outside. Their white robes had to mean they were saints, but what on earth were they doing? They each sat on a bench in the courtyard outside, chatting idly as servants drew well water and poured it into jars. The servants added some green liquid from another container to the jars of well water, capped and shook the jars, and finally handed them to the saints.

The saints then laid down on their benches—which seemed rather improper for ladies—whispered something with the jars on their chests, and immediately got back to their chatter. Shortly after, the jars began to glow faintly, prompting the servants to collect them.

Are they...doing what I think they're doing?

The butler who greeted me at the entrance returned with a tray of jars filled with clear, sparkling liquid—the very same jars the saints had held.

"Thank you very much," I said with a bow.

I felt down as I walked back with the jars.

Maybe they modernized the process? A lot can change in three hundred years. I can see them needing to streamline the process, especially with fewer saints around now. Yeah, this is just the new norm...the new...norm...

But no matter how much I tried to reassure myself, I couldn't deny the truth. It rose up in my memory, vivid and vital.

There was power in nature.

It rested in the teeming forests of verdant green, in the myriad flowers blooming in full glory, even in the roots that snaked throughout the earth. It gave nature the tenacity to rise again when trampled underfoot or blanketed by snow, this undeterrable need to grow.

Nature was abundant with power. What if someone took that abundance into the human body?

That question is what birthed the healing potion.

Three hundred years ago, saints often visited natural springs. These springs were always enclosed in a plethora of flora: trees, flowers, and—most importantly—medicinal herbs. With their love for nature singing in their hearts, the saints would pluck those herbs, draw the spring water, and add the herbs to the mixture. They would then pour their magic into the resulting concoction, bound with a wish that those ailing could share the abundant power of nature and recover. As they weaved their spells, the herbs melted away and the water began to sparkle, creating a healing potion that always took on the same color as the herbs—a deep, verdant green.

So why were modern healing potions transparent?

I peered at the healing potions I'd just received. *Was the process now so different that a part of the effect is gone? Oh! The pain-dulling effect must be missing from these new potions*—that's *why the one I drank hurt me so badly!* I remembered back to drinking the healing potion and shuddered. *I'm never touching that stuff again, even if I get hurt!*

Nodding fervently to myself, I set off for the familiar stables.

I stood in front of a detached building adjacent to the Fourth Monster Tamer Knight Brigade headquarters. I figured this had to be the place? I looked around, saw what looked like the caretaker's office, and gave the door a knock.

"Excuse me! Fia Ruud here! I'm in charge of giving the familiars their healing potions, starting today!"

A well-built man in his late forties opened the door. "Oh, so you're the one. Patty already caught me up to speed. How 'bout I show you around?"

Together, we entered the stable. It was a long, rectangular building with a high ceiling. Three rows of cages lined the walls, each containing a single monster.

"This building here is our biggest stable, housing the familiars that are D-rank and below. One stable over, you'll find the C-rank familiars; another over and you'll find our B-ranks. The ones past that are empty." The caretaker frowned for a moment but continued, "The familiars might scare you a bit now, but they actually get lonely. Believe it or not, they like to be pampered. Cute, right? But they get real nasty if left alone, so their masters always come running when called. You can even see some knights here now."

"Aw, that *is* cute." True enough, I could see knights here and there, talking to and petting their familiars. But mixed in with the rugged knights was one white-robed girl who seemed out of place. "Who's that girl?"

"A saint." The caretaker smiled. "Only knights of the Fourth Monster Tamer Knight Brigade and saints are allowed in the stables. The knights, as you can imagine, come to look after their familiars, but the saints are also allowed in to heal them. But she's the only one who actually visits."

The young saint stood in front of the cage, staring at the familiar inside. She looked around seven or eight years old, with orange hair that reached her shoulders. Her facial features were cute and childish.

Why did she come here? Hmm. For now, I had to put that thought aside and listen to the caretaker's explanation.

"Your job is to make the injured familiars drink healing potions," he said. "One jar should last 'em about three days, so after that you'll need to fetch more from the saints."

Oh, that's good! I don't need to make the trip every day. But... can this jar really last three days?

"That healing potion's for human use, so you're going to need to water it down to nine parts water, one part healing potion.

Monsters have higher natural recovery than humans, y'see. The injured monsters are the ones with a red card above their nameplate."

Sure enough, there was a twenty-centimeter nameplate on each cage inscribed with the monster and master's names. Above each nameplate was a pocket holding cards for some sort of marking system.

"You just pour the diluted healing potion onto each plate and push it through the cage's opening. The hard part is after that..." he sighed, pointing to a cage. "The familiars have been ordered by their masters to drink the healing potion, but...the taste is awful, and the pain is terrible. They never drink it obediently. Most of the monsters will try to intimidate you, so you need to stand firm and keep reminding them they need to drink. It's their master's order, after all."

"I...see."

The caretaker scratched his head, picking his words carefully now. "Every, uh...every now and then, you'll have a familiar that just won't listen. They size up the one feeding them and just decide that they're not strong enough to obey. So usually, you see, the Fourth Monster Tamer Knight Brigade assigns the task to a rotation of their most intimidating knights. So. Um. Good luck."

Oh...that's why Patty was so against me doing this task. She even stood up to her superior over it. How nice of her. Okay, if I find Patty's familiar, I'll take extra good care of it!

I thanked the caretaker and got to work.

Now that I could get a good look, I noticed that there were quite a few different types of monsters in the cages. *Um, I believe he said this stable was only D-rank and below?* I scanned the area looking for the cages with red cards out—and there we go!

A violet boar! The familiar boar-type monster sat inside its cage, marked with a red card. It must've been injured recently; a bandage wrapped across its midsection was spotted with blood.

Get well soon, buddy, I thought, pouring the healing potion into the plate.

Immediately, the violet boar stood on its rear legs and let out a monstrous roar. "Graaaoooh!" It nearly touched the cage, snarling and bearing its tusks.

"Drink it," I said, gazing into its eyes. "It tastes gross and may hurt, but it'll make you better. I'm sure your master would want nothing more."

But the familiar simply bared its teeth and growled.

Oh dear. Now what am I supposed to do?

While the healing potion did taste terrible and cause pain, they needed it to heal. I couldn't just let them refuse because they didn't like it. But I also didn't want to excite the familiar anymore and risk opening that wound on its abdomen.

I pushed the plate forward a little more when the familiar grazed the back of my hand through the bars with one of its tusks.

Ah...I could heal this in an instant, I suppose...

Zavilia popped his head out, noticing my troubles. **"Can I help, Fia?"**

"Huh? Um, sure?" I stammered.

He emitted a low wail, and the familiar in front of me froze. Then it took a few steps forward and drank the healing potion obediently.

"Huh? Wh—can you...can you control monsters?!"

"No, I believe that is impossible. I merely gave it a warning cry. Most monsters submit when they hear my unique voice."

"Whoa...that's awesome! You're like the king of monsters!" I meant it as praise, but Zavilia seemed to stiffen in surprise.

"Sorry, but...I'm no king."

"Huh? I didn't mean it literally. Just, like, you're very kingly! You don't have to be a *real* king!"

"Fia...do you want me to be a king?"

"Hmm..." I looked at Zavilia. His icy eyes looking straight back at me from beneath his fluffy, blue exterior. "You're cute and strong and gentle and wonderful! I think you're fine as you are now! Besides, you can't just wish your way into becoming a king! But even if you were destined to be a king, we'd just figure it out when it came up!"

"Yeah...thank you, Fia," Zavilia nuzzled against my face.

Aww. So cute! "All right, should we finish with the rest of the familiars?" I said to Zavilia.

A meek and lovely voice rang out behind me. "Excuse me... Miss Knight?"

I turned around to find the young saint from earlier before me, hands clenching her robe.

"Hello, Your Grace." I replied, bending over to her eye level.

She hesitated, as if unsure what to say. Her bright orange hair was glossy, and her cheeks were the rosy color of a little kid's. She was pretty adorable up close!

I waited for her to find the words to speak, and after a short wait, she did. "Um... Miss Knight is amazing! Even though you're not their master, you can make the monsters drink the potion without even threatening them."

"Miss Knight? No, Fia!" She looked at me, confused. I elaborated with a smile. "I mean, my name is Fia. You can just call me that if you like."

She blushed. "Oh, m-my name is Charlotte. Um, please call me that...if you'd like."

"Very well. Miss Charlotte then?"

"N-no, just Charlotte is fine! A-and, um, you don't have to be all formal. You can talk to me like family or something."

Hmm? Aren't saints practically worshiped and treated super formally all the time? I looked at Charlotte and saw her gripping her robe just above her knees, trembling and teary-eyed. *Wh-what is this creature?! Cuteness overload!*

"Charlotte it is, then!"

She smiled broadly, but suddenly tears started falling from her eyes.

"Huh? I-is something wrong?" Surprised, I held out a hand to her. She grabbed on to it.

"Nobody uses the name Mommy gave me... They just call me

'Your Grace.' But that's not my name..." Her tears moistened the cuffs of my uniform.

I hugged her tight and gently patted her back. "I see. I'm guessing they found out you were a saint when you were, what, three years old?"

She nodded, her face still buried in my chest. "Because I'm a saint, they said I couldn't be with Mommy and took me to the church. They said I could meet Mommy again if I became a good saint, but I...I can't. My saint power is weak. I can't make healing potions... Mommy must be ashamed of me..."

Finally overwhelmed, she started crying in earnest. I kept on patting her back, but...her words struck me as odd.

It wasn't always the case, but orange hair often meant that somebody was well suited to be a saint. Spirits made pacts because they were drawn to the blood of saints, so it was said that saints with red hair—the color of blood—carried the greatest potential power. Orange hair was close to red, so it should've been up there too. But was her talent as a saint was so low that she couldn't use it?

After holding her and patting her back for a while, Charlotte calmed down. Her tears stopped, she looked up at me sheepishly, and that was when she spotted Zavilia—he'd climbed onto my shoulder.

"A bluebird! Mommy always said they bring happiness."

I smiled and stroked her head. "Your mommy's right. So many happy things have happened to me since I met this bluebird, and you know what? I'm sure happy things are coming your way too." I took her hand. "I still have to feed healing potions to the injured monsters. Will you help me?"

She beamed up at me. "Yeah!"

The rest of the feeding went without a hitch; as soon as Zavilia gave his warning cry, the familiars obediently lapped up the healing potion...even if they all collapsed and started groaning shortly after drinking the stuff.

I know it hurts. I'm sorry.

I knew how that pain felt, after all. The healing magic of the potion flowed through every nook and cranny of the body, bringing overwhelming agony with it as an unfortunate side effect.

Something gripped my hand tight. I looked over to see Charlotte watching the familiars with tears in her eyes. She was a gentle soul, sympathizing with their pain. Yeah, she was definitely meant to be a saint.

"Charlotte, are you free right now? Why don't we go for a walk?" I remembered there being a natural spring on the east side, within the castle walls.

"Okay!"

The sunlight was nice and warm. We walked together, hand in hand, while Zavilia perched on my shoulder. Several springs came into sight as we reached our destination. I looked over each one before finally coming to a decision.

I stared into the waters of the tiniest spring in the area, and Charlotte peered at her reflection. "This one's just small enough,"

I said to myself. "It'll do." I turned to Charlotte. "Now then, how about we practice healing magic together?"

"Huh? But I..." Charlotte clamped up and looked down at her feet.

"Hee hee, it's all right. Not like I can tell how you're doing anyway—I can't use healing magic or anything." I met her gaze with a smile as she looked back up at me. "But practice means failing a lot, so go ahead and fail away as much as you'd like."

I gripped her hand tight. She gripped back and nodded. Together, we picked some of the medicinal herbs growing nearby and dropped them into the spring.

"These herbs look lovely. I bet you they're super good for you too," I said.

Charlotte had a good eye; she could discern the medicinal herbs from the rest of the plants without a problem. As for Zavilia, he left his usual roost—my uniform—and took a nap on the grass.

I didn't know how much time had passed. Once I thought there were enough herbs in the small spring, I called out to Charlotte. "Okay, roll up your sleeves and put your hands in, then pour out your healing magic. We're going to make some healing potions for practice, okay?"

"Huh? But...the other saints use dried herbs, already all crushed up and dissolved in water. And this spring is too big for me too..." Her shaky voice trailed off.

"Hee hee, don't worry, it's just practice. Give it a shot." After she rolled up her sleeves, I took her hands in mine. I touched my forehead to hers as we put our hands into the spring.

"Try pouring your healing magic out," I said.

Nervous as she was, she gave it a try. Soon enough, she'd created a small, slow-going stream of magic.

Hmm...her magic flow isn't very good. I guess she doesn't use healing magic much; I can sense parts of her body where the flow is still a little jammed. You'd normally just sweep this kind of thing away with practice, but...whatever, I'll just send her a little magic and clear it away myself.

"Um...huh?" Charlotte blinked. "I...I can feel my magic flowing."

I smiled and let go of her hands. "Very good. Now direct that magic into the spring. Slowly steer the magic flowing through your body into your hands, little by little. Got it? Now, look at the spring. It's beautiful, isn't it? Can you see the fresh herbs we threw in? Try directing your magic towards that."

Gradually, magic flowed from Charlotte's fingertips and into the spring.

Hee hee, I knew it! You're well on your way to becoming a wonderful saint, Charlotte.

"Yep, just like that. Now, think of the injured familiars that were crying in pain. You want to help them, right? Well, this water has absorbed the power of the earth for a long time, and these herbs have absorbed the power of nature. Let's borrow that power. Let the magic flow from you as you think of how happy those familiars will be when they drink your healing potion."

I closed my eyes as I spoke, slowly pouring my own magic in as well. "Very good, Charlotte, but it seems like your left hand is releasing more than your right. Do you think you can balance them?"

Slowly, bit by bit, Charlotte brought her magic under finer control. Eventually, my own magic ran dry, and we were left with our finished product—a bright, sparkling spring. The herbs had dissolved, tinting the clear spring water a gorgeous green.

"Ah...beautiful. The color of healing," I said proudly. But then I noticed Charlotte...she sounded like she was about to cry.

"F-Fia, my body feels...weird? It feels warm, like there's this kinda energy flowing in me..."

I tousled her hair gently. "Congratulations, Charlotte. That's healing magic. Thanks to you, *alllll* of this spring's water has turned into healing potion!" I grinned and spread my arms out wide towards the spring.

"Huh?" Charlotte's mouth hung open.

"Hm. I get it," Zavilia muttered from his spot in the grass. **"You just want to stop thinking and escape reality... I suppose I'll pretend to be asleep for just a little longer."**

Charlotte just stood there frozen, mouth agape. "The spring's...been turned into healing potion?" she said, stupefied. She shook her head. "U-um, Fia? I'm sorry, but healing potion isn't green. This is something else. It has to be..."

"Ehe heh, those clear ones are failed healing potions. This is

the real deal!" I said with a smug smile, but Charlotte didn't look convinced.

As for Zavilia, he was still lying on the grass pretending to be asleep.

Hmm? This isn't the reaction I was expecting. I took a small vial out of my pocket, filled it with the spring water, and then picked Zavilia up. "Let's go eat lunch for now. I used up all my mag—er, my stamina, so I'm starving!"

"Your magic never ceases to amaze me," Zavilia muttered from within my uniform. **"You've dried up all of your own magic, and yet you haven't taken a single drop of it from me. Just what have you done to achieve such perfect control over your power?"**

"Um, Charlotte, I'm sorry for keeping you so long, but would you care to join me for lunch? I was thinking we could go back to the familiar stables and feed the familiars this new healing potion afterwards."

"Okay!" she replied, clutching my hand tight. *Ahh! So cute!*

Charlotte managed to control her magic output; she probably still had twenty or thirty percent of her magic left, so she wasn't as exhausted as I was. Still, I'd already kept her past lunchtime, and every meal was important for a growing child.

I always get too engrossed in things and forget about the consequences... I really gotta do something about that bad habit of mine.

The two of us arrived at the canteen, largely empty since we arrived after the normal lunch hour.

Charlotte and I had just sat down opposite each other when a familiar voice called out to me.

"Oh, Fia!" I turned to find Fabian standing there holding a tray.

"Late lunch?" I asked.

"Mm-hmm. I was working on something for the vice-captain, so my lunch got pushed back. But it was all worthwhile—I got to run into you, after all." Fabian turned to face Charlotte. "It is a pleasure to make your acquaintance, Your Grace. I am Fabian Wyner of the First Knight Brigade. May I join you for lunch?"

Charlotte nodded, and Fabian sat down next to me. "I heard you were working with the Fourth Monster Tamer Knight Brigade," he said. "Does that somehow involve being with Her Grace? And, uh, did you eat too much? Your stomach is bulging..."

"All you knights need a vision test, I swear. Does this look like my real stomach to you? What is it, do you all just work yourselves so hard your brains fall out of your heads? This bulge under my clothes happens to be my familiar, thank you very much. And I'm with Charlotte because we were doing some special practice together."

"I...didn't know you even *had* a familiar," he said, exasperated. "And here you are, close enough to Her Grace that you can call her by her name. You really are full of surprises, Fia. You leave my sight for a moment and I find out you've done the unimaginable. But at least you look well. Captain Cyril was worried about how the Fourth Monster Tamer Knight Brigade might welcome you. Actually, Captain Cyril's been looking rather tired lately. It'd be nice if you could come back soon to ease his worrying."

I tilted my head in wonder as I chewed my meat. *Just what could leave Captain Cyril so tired? Ohh, maybe it was that person who insulted him directly? I guess that's still bothering him, then. He seems like he's always trying his best, so I bet he's pretty thin-skinned about that kinda stuff.*

Fabian clearly felt bad for only talking to me, so he flashed a dazzling smile at Charlotte and began making small talk. Charlotte blushed and kept her replies short.

Not even Charlotte is immune to that blinding smile. Fabian's just on a whole 'nother level...

Soon enough, we parted ways with Fabian and walked hand-in-hand back to the familiar stables. My steps were lighter now that my body had recovered from magic fatigue.

Wait, what? How? Shouldn't I be out of magic? Why does it feel like half of it is back? I looked down my collar at Zavilia. *I see...you must've given me some of your magic. Thanks, little guy.*

The familiars all stared at us as we entered their stables. The tips of their noses pressed against the cages as they let out soft, wheedling whines.

"Um, Charlotte?! Any idea what's going on?"

"N-no, I've never seen them like this."

The two of us took a step back, overwhelmed by the strange welcome.

O...kay? Still, I can't just up and leave. There's work to be done!

I poured the healing potion Charlotte had made earlier onto a plate and put it inside one injured familiar's cage. I was just about to ask Zavilia to help out when, to my surprise, the monster began drinking without hesitation.

Huh? What's going on?

Zavilia whispered up to me from inside of my uniform. **"When you used healing magic earlier, that magic flowed through and healed parts of your body. Your healed body gives off a sweet smell reminiscent of saint's blood, a smell that monsters adore. It makes them hunger for saint-flesh. But ah, don't worry! That is not the case for monsters who've made pacts with humans. They merely want your attention...and pampering."**

"Ohhhh...hmm." Come to think of it, I hadn't bothered healing that scratch the violet boar left on me. I could still see some of the blood on my arm, in fact. Also, after Zavilia had accidentally lashed out at me and left me bleeding out, he'd protected me from a whole lot of monsters. And he *had* mentioned the smell of blood back then...

But I don't remember monsters reacting like that in my previous life...

"You had a pact with spirits in your past life, did you not? They surely helped you somehow."

I see. They did so much for me behind the scenes...

We did a round through the stables, feeding the green healing potion to the injured familiars. Every one of them was meek and obedient, acting like pampered pets and making soft wheedling sounds.

W-weird? But...cute!

This time, none of the familiars appeared to be in any pain.

Charlotte noticed that. "Um, Fia? I really don't think this green water is healing potion. If it was, they'd be hurting."

"Heh heh, I'm sure it's healing potion! You just don't know how incredible you are yet. How about we come back tomorrow to check on them?"

We made a promise to see the familiars the next morning and parted ways.

That night, a brilliant craft idea for Zavilia hit me like a ton of bricks, and I just *had* to give it a try. It took some work, but soon enough I was holding up my new creation proudly. I then laid down quietly next to Zavilia—didn't want to wake him up, after all.

Before I fell asleep, I remembered what Fabian had said. *Captain Cyril's so tired these days, right? I hope he's okay. It'd be nice if he could at least get a good night's sleep...*

My thoughts faded, and I slept like a baby.

A Tale of the
Secret
Saint

Desmond, Captain of the Second Knight Brigade

MY NAME IS Desmond Ronan, captain of the Second Knight Brigade. Last year, being the eldest son, I became the head of the Ronan family. Our family holds the rank of earl, a high-level aristocratic title.

There I was, the eldest son of an earl family, the captain of a brigade, attractive enough, and well built. Obviously, I've been popular with the fairer sex since a young age. So why in the world did my long-time fiancée abandon me for my younger brother?

My younger brother—a man who wouldn't inherit the title of earl, a man with a bog-standard appearance, a low-ranking civil servant with a feeble body.

I, of all people, was second choice to *that*?

Was there something wrong with me? Something that I couldn't see, something beneath the surface that drove people away? Or were *they* the problem—that two-faced fairer sex, that horde of backstabbers?

Without a moment's hesitation, I chose to believe the latter. I have not regretted it since.

"If you could have one person by your side on the battlefield, who would it be?"

A foolish question: it would surely be Cyril Sutherland, captain of the First Knight Brigade.

Those who reach the peak of their art often made said art look easy, and Cyril was such a case; with a sword, he was perfection itself. From a distance, his fighting seemed like nothing more than incredibly plain, basic swordsmanship. His blade always took the path of least resistance through the enemy's vitals, never deviating, always favoring quickness over flash.

And when his fighting spirit ignited, a faint smile rose to his face. He was without equal in that state, a state that would not end until there were no more foes to cut down. That smile of his...we called it "The Smile of Death." The sight of that smile brought cheers from his allies. It was a sign that victory was guaranteed.

That same unparalleled fighter was equally talented in matters of state. His rich education from an early age made paperwork a breeze for him. However, it seemed that he was now in a rut of sorts, and so his subordinates came to me for help. Knowing the reason for his rut, I decided to check up on him.

Cyril and I met for a clandestine meeting in the recreation

room of the Royal Castle, the one set aside for captain and vice-captains. The two of us shared the room alone that night, save for the waiter. We didn't so much as look at the chessboards and billiard tables, electing to drink the night away.

Cyril downed his amber drink and ordered another. Drank that, ordered another.

I couldn't stop myself. "You could save time by ordering a few drinks at once, if you're going to go through them so fast."

Cyril gave me a look from beneath his long eyelashes. "I'd never be so crass."

That right? I supposed that dukes always had to worry about appearance.

I shrugged and reached for my own glass. "I get it. Sometimes a man's gotta drink. I'll stick with you tonight, so you can feel free to put 'em away."

"Ha ha...it's not like you to be so sympathetic. I'll take you up on that offer." He closed his eyes. "I'm in the mood to drink myself ragged." There was a tinge of self-derision in his voice.

"You? Drunk? You're the only person I know who can drink like a fish and be all right the next morning." I emptied my glass and ordered another. But if he was really set on it...

Then I'll match you drink for drink today. You needed to be either very brave or very stupid to try to drink Cyril under the table, and I was feeling a little bit of both.

He took no notice of my bravado. "And here I thought you were being sympathetic. You could be a little kinder, you know? I'm actually quite depressed right now."

I know. It'd do you good to stop bottling it all up inside—I suspect that's why you're miserable. But you won't open up to me tonight for damn certain, so I might as well poke fun at you.

"What a coincidence," I said. "I'm depressed too. My pride's in shambles thanks to that recruit of yours. *Ohhh*, my entire career as commandant of the military police has all been for naught! Whatever shall I do with my life?"

Cyril was no idiot. He knew I was just messing around, and he'd play along if it meant he didn't have to share his own feelings. "You know," he began, "many of the knights idolize you—the bachelors especially. You've got the status and you've got the looks. You're a hard worker. But for all of that, you swore off love after your younger brother snatched away your fiancée. Great, isn't it? I mean, you may not be popular with women, but the single men adore you."

"Wha—hold on, what's *that* about? There was an insult hidden in there!"

Cyril smiled defeatedly. Emptied his glass. Ordered another. "I envy how much people respect you. That's what I'm trying to say. Especially after my direct subordinate called me 'horrible' to my face."

"Ahhh. Well, ah...that wasn't strictly...directed *at* you."

"You're...you're right, yes, but it's affecting me all the same." He leaned into his chair, crossed his legs, and rested his head on the back for a moment. He closed his eyes.

I watched him silently, finished my glass, and ordered more. *You're lying, Cyril. That's not what's bothering you.* I found myself sinking back into my chair as well, crossing my legs and folding my arms. I let out a heavy sigh.

The royal family had a bizarre obsession with saints, enough to spend a few hundred years glorifying them. When Fia insulted those who had twisted what it meant to be a saint, that criticism extended to the royal family. That included Cyril, as he had a right to the throne. I could tell that Fia herself hadn't *intended* to do that, but the words were said all the same.

I brought my new drink to my lips and glanced at Cyril. He still sat back, eyes closed.

I've never seen someone fall in love at first sight. But I suppose I've seen the moment a few words rip a man's heart to shreds.

Cyril had revered saints since the moment he was born. Any warrior knew just how miraculous and vital healing was, and Cyril was a hero; he'd fought across countless battlefields alongside the captain. Nobody knew the importance of the saints more than him, and nobody had reflected upon them as often and as deeply as he.

And although he'd never dared to say it, he felt that something was wrong with the saints. More than anyone, he sensed the disparity between the royal family's image of the saints and the saints themselves. That disparity had tormented him for so long... and then she'd come along.

"Hey, Captain...how do you feel about the saints? Do you want to worship them like gods?"

She laughed at the very idea.

"Heh heh, no...of course not. Saints aren't a bunch of distant, fickle gods. No, the saints are the shield of the knights."

And the moment those words left her mouth, I could see it plain on Cyril's face: the look of a man whose heart had been ripped to shreds.

Or perhaps not. Perhaps it was the pain and ecstasy of a man facing a divine revelation.

Her words must've been the answer he sought. The answer he'd searched for alone for a lifetime, stated plainly by a giggling young girl who seemed amused by our inability to understand something so simple.

I had a feeling Cyril would cling to her answer for the rest of his life. No matter what he heard, no matter what he felt—from now on her words would be his truth. He had found his purpose as a knight.

"That girl is really something..." I muttered without realizing.

She'd found her way into the guarded hearts of us knights and anchored herself deep.

Cyril hadn't once brought up what Fia said about how saints were supposed to be, which was proof enough that the shock was still too deep, the matter too personal. All he would offer was that Fia had made light of him—a petty complaint to distract from his real worries.

I could only guess what Cyril saw on that moonlit night. Did he see a drunken girl, smiling as she staggered along humming, barefoot with boots in hand? Or did he see something else entirely?

I clearly remembered my own drunken thoughts at the sight of Cyril's face: *Hah! And that's why you don't trust women!*

"Indeed..." Cyril replied. "Not just anyone would make an insult in front of a superior like that." But he understood what I truly meant.

Fine. I'll play along if you're not ready to talk about it.

We talked intermittently as we drank glass after glass. A long, considered silence fell over us. "The captain..." said Cyril, picking his words carefully. Then, suddenly, he shook his head. "Ah, never mind."

Oh, right, of course. The one person who reveres the saints even more than Cyril—Captain Saviz. I shuddered. Just how badly could a single girl shake up the knight brigades?

"Cyril, let's drink! If I don't get straight plastered now, I'm going to lose my damn mind!"

"Wonderful idea, Desmond. Let's see if you can get me drunk tonight!"

You? Drunk? Hah! All the alcohol in the room wouldn't be enough! Not that I'd dare to say that aloud.

We drank until morning. The end result: I crashed half-dead in the early hours, while Cyril looked and acted as normal as ever. I let out a small groan as the morning sun shone into the room.

"Don't give me that look, Cyril...you're the odd one. Your tolerance for alcohol is positively inhuman. So don't look at me like I'm a pile of human garbage, all right?"

Some thanks. Even though I'd gone out of my way to drink with him, Cyril wouldn't stop giving me that patronizing look of his!

A Tale of the
Secret Saint

18
The Fourth Monster Tamer Knight Brigade Part 2

IRST THING the next morning, I waited excitedly for Zavilia to wake up. He had a habit of shifting about in his sleep, always ending up right on top of my stomach when I woke up even if he'd started the night under the blanket. The Blue Dove disguise probably wasn't enough to keep him warm at night, I realized. So I'd crafted some new, cozy outerwear for him the previous night.

I couldn't wait to surprise him! I stared at him expectantly, waiting for him to wake up. A little while later, he finally started to stir, nuzzling his head against my belly.

Aww...I wonder what you're dreaming about.

I stared at him for some time until his eyes fluttered open. **"Good morning, Fia... Is something the matter?"**

"Eh heh heh! It may be spring, but it's still pretty chilly in the morning, right?"

"I get the impression that you want me to say yes, but...I already have this wonderful Blue Dove disguise. I couldn't possibly ask you to make me anything more."

"My, aren't you a humble little darling! That's good—the humble ones always get the big rewards in the end."

"Ah...I see. The outcome was already predetermined, no matter what answer I gave..." Zavilia slumped onto the bed defeatedly, his tail swishing back and forth. **"Oh. Goodness. Dearie me. It's ever so cold every morning. If only there was something that would help."**

He sounded a bit deadpan for some reason, but it was still the right answer. "Well, Zavilia, you're in luck! *Ta-da!* I made special outerwear just for you!" I proudly showed him the product of last night's efforts.

"Um...it appears that you've made another Blue Dove disguise, but...much worse?"

"No, silly. It's outerwear. I made it to fit over what you're wearing right now for when it's cold!" I spread my creation out in front of him so he could see it better. "Look, I sewed the leftover Blue Dove feathers in. I didn't have enough, so it's a bit patchy, but I used two layers of cloth for warmth to make up for that."

I continued by explaining the special hole I left for the tail. "Now, you're probably thinking 'Hey, Fia! Why use all those Blue Dove feathers if you're just making an extra layer to keep me warm!' Is that right?"

"...Sure."

"But there's a method to my madness! Watch: if I put my hand through this hole I left for the tail...*ta-da*! It becomes a Blue Dove puppet!" I put my hand through the tail hole and began puppeting the outerwear. The outerwear's head cover looked like a proper head, making it look like a second Blue Dove next to Zavilia.

Zavilia took a deep breath in. **"Right. I don't think such a feature is...strictly necessary. When would you ever need a puppet?"**

"Don't puppets kinda justify themselves? Um...maybe when you're sad I can use it to cheer you up? Oh, now that I'm friends with Charlotte, I can use it with her. I'm pretty sure kids like these soft plushie kinda things."

"True, she is around that age. But you should probably explain that it's outerwear doubling as a Blue Dove puppet before you show her. It's a bit hard to...*ahem*...parse at first look."

Oho! Explain, then show. Duly noted. I placed the puppet on my left hand and held Zavilia up to my chest. "Let's show Charlotte later when we do our healing potion feeding. Oh, but first, I need to report to the Fourth Monster Tamer Knight Brigade captain's office..."

Gideon would want to know whether his orders were being carried out properly, I figured. Besides, I had time to kill before I had to meet up with Charlotte.

I knocked on the door of the captain's office.

"Come in."

"Excuse me," I said as I entered. I saw Gideon slouched on a chair with Patty by his side, holding some documents.

"Good morning, Fia. Need something?" Patty asked.

"Good morning, Patty. I just came by to report that yesterday's healing potion feeding went without a hitch."

"That's great. I was worried it'd be too difficult for you, so I sent a few knights to check on you yesterday evening. They said it looked like all the familiars drank healing potion. You did a great job, as expected of someone recommended by the First Knight Brigade captain," Patty said with a smile.

I was about to reply when Gideon interrupted with a scoff. "Look at you, getting all excited over a simple task like feeding healing potion to the familiars. Must be easy being a First Knight Brigade elite—it's not like we in the Fourth Monster Tamer Knight Brigade are so busy with urgent work that we hardly slept."

Ah...he's in a bad mood again. "Good morning, Vice-Captain Gideon. The truth is, I also didn't sleep much last night. I was making some warm clothes for my darling little familiar. As vice-captain of the Fourth Monster Tamer Knight Brigade, I'm sure you understand how important that is."

"*Hmph*. Not bad. I can see why your familiar likes you so much. The thing made it quite *loudly clear* to me yesterday. But you obviously stayed up so you could brag about it to me, you brownnosing little snot!"

"Huh? Okay, you're just biased against me!" I blurted. "If a knight of your brigade told you the same thing, you'd praise them!"

Patty giggled. "Vice-Captain Gideon, I could swear you were telling everyone about how much you loved caring for your familiar not too long ago. Is that bragging too?"

Gideon shot Patty a sharp glare, but she met his gaze coolly. There was a brief silence, broken a moment later by a knock on the door.

"Come in!" Gideon bellowed.

I looked up to see Cyril step in, wearing a dazzling white uniform with a touch of black—the uniform only worn by vice-captains or higher. The white symbolized faith and integrity. His captain sash draped across his shoulder, and the epaulettes and aiguillette of his uniform glittered underneath. His uniform hugged his well-built body; combined with his excellent posture, he was the perfect image of an imposing, high-ranking commanding officer.

Gideon hurried to his feet. At that, Cyril raised a hand and flashed a friendly smile. "Pardon me for visiting so early in the morning. I'm just here to check on how my knight is doing. Please, be at ease." He faced me now and smiled sweetly. "Are you enjoying your time here? I hope you're almost finished; I'd like to bring you back to the First Knight Brigade soon."

Aww, how nice! He came all this way just to check up on me! "Well, I fed all the injured familiars healing potion, so they should be healed by tomorrow."

Cyril looked baffled. "What are you talking about? I temporarily assigned you to the Fourth Monster Tamer Knight Brigade to determine the health of the familiars. What does that have to do with feeding them healing potion?"

"Huh? Ohhh, that. Um...well?"

That plan was squashed the moment I met Vice-Captain Gideon, sir. But if I said that, it'd just cause a huge fight between Cyril and Gideon. *Umm...let's just try to change the subject!*

"Uh, well, in answer to your great question about whether I'm enjoying my time here, which is a great question, why...yes! Yes, I am! I met up with my familiar and Patty's really nice, and—"

"That's enough. Tell me later." Cyril cut me off and turned to Gideon. He maintained his calm visage as he directed questions towards the vice-captain. "How interesting. It would *seem* my knight here hasn't even *begun* the task I sent her to do. You wouldn't happen to know the reason, would you?"

"Whuhham..." Gideon opened his mouth, but no proper words came out.

Cyril waited for some time. He then tilted his head to the side slightly, perhaps irritated by the lack of an answer. "It isn't a complicated question. Either she neglected her duties or someone in the Fourth Monster Tamer Knight Brigade prevented her from fulfilling them."

Cyril stopped and stared at Gideon, perhaps waiting for an answer again. None came. Cyril continued. "At any rate, you are the one temporarily in charge. Is that correct? As such, you have a responsibility to fix any problems that arise. So, as the bearer of that responsibility, would you kindly tell me why my knight didn't fulfill her orders?"

He crossed his arms.

"Guhhf...?" Another unintelligible noise.

"That reminds me," said Cyril. "I heard you shouting from the other side of the door just now. Might I ask who you were shouting at?"

"Er..."

"Were you shouting at your assistant here? Or perhaps you

were shouting at Fia. What terrible mistake did she make for you to yell at her so?"

"Um..." Gideon's mouth flapped ridiculously, trying to form words but instead gasping frantically.

Once again, Cyril waited patiently for a response. After some time passed without one, he just smiled defeatedly, raised his foot slightly and dropped it on the low table to his side.

The low table split in two with a loud *crunch*.

"Wha, uh?!" Gideon made a startled noise and looked down at the mess below. Cyril had hardly lifted his foot to smash the low table. Just how strong were his legs?

Smiling, Cyril approached Gideon, grabbed him by the collar, and pulled his face close. The ghastly smile didn't move a bit as he said, "A question: Have you been misusing the knight *I* personally sent you for a specific task? A *second* question: Would you prefer official discipline, or would you rather I crush your head like a rotten melon?"

His face was frightening despite his perfect smile, but not as frightening as the fact that he held both the authority and might to carry out either of those threats without a second thought.

Gideon turned pale, but with great effort began to speak. "I-I-I-I've..."

Even from a distance away, I could see his teeth chattering. *Yikes. That's pure fear right there. I suppose being the captain of the First Knight Brigade means that Cyril has to command with an iron fist. He could probably get away with doing basically anything in the name of disciplinary action too. Scary.*

Gideon fell silent again, opting to simply quake in his boots. I did feel bad for him. I mean, he said a lot of terrible things to me, but I didn't hate the guy. I didn't *like* him either, of course, but his insults were nothing compared to the ones I got from my brother Leon, let alone the insults from my three brothers in my previous life. Compared to them, nothing Gideon or Leon had ever said to me could really make me see them as *bad*. Besides, watching Cyril go after Gideon felt like watching an adult pick on a scared kid.

With a deep sigh, I decided I'd step in to help Gideon, although part of me didn't want to. I was about to say something when the door opened again. I turned around to find a knight I had never seen before standing there.

Gideon took one glance at the mystery man before going limp with relief and exclaiming in a weak, hoarse voice, "C-Captain Quentin!"

The knight named Quentin glanced at Gideon, then his eyes settled on me. He was tall and broad, with dark brown skin and glossy black hair. The image of a certain large, nimble cat came to mind the moment I laid eyes on him.

A handsome Tiger, a gorgeous Dragon, and now...wow, that's one good-lookin' panther. I couldn't stop myself from staring.

Quentin grimaced and ran a hand through his curly hair. "Give me a break. I take a short leave and suddenly there are two calamity-class monsters in my office?"

He seemed a little wary of us. He kept his distance and left his guard up.

Quentin, Captain of the Fourth Monster Tamer Knight Brigade

I AM QUENTIN AGUTTER, captain of the Fourth Monster Tamer Knight Brigade. Our brigade is a little different from the others—we fight alongside our familiars.

The process of taming monsters into familiars was only discovered around a hundred years ago, so it's still an underdeveloped field. Because of that, giving orders to our familiars never works perfectly...which can be dangerous in a fight.

If only my familiar hadn't retreated. If only my familiars worked together to attack. So many "if onlys" as our familiars strayed from our orders and gave unsatisfactory results. And we, the knights of the Fourth Monster Tamer Knight Brigade, struggled with that every day.

Despite caring for our familiars carefully and training alongside them daily, we simply couldn't get the results we needed in combat. Each failure made our familiars look worse. The other brigades looked down on us; even if monster taming was a developing field, results were everything.

I couldn't fault them, either—results *were* everything on the battlefield, where the alternative to results was often death. But the scorn from the other brigades left my knights alternating between distrust and resentment. Before long, they were consumed by animosity. My vice-captain, Gideon, was one of the most outspoken in his hate for the other brigades. He wasn't a bad man, he was simply frank about his feelings to a fault. His strong sense of justice was tempered by his impulsivity and temper. The man had a bad habit of jumping to the worst conclusions about other people, in a way that only ended up hurting him in the end.

His performance was fine under my supervision, but when I left on a special mission for a time, that left him in command of the brigade. I made Patty his assistant as insurance, of course, but I was still worried.

I could only hope he'd do all right in my absence...

My special mission was from the captain himself: capture the Black King. There were three Great Beasts with influence over this continent, and one of them was thought to have disappeared half a year ago.

We received a report of a red dragon flying above Blackpeak Mountain, a sacred place at the northern tip of the continent. The red dragon landed there and then took off again shortly after. Blackpeak Mountain had been the territory of the Black King for centuries, and no other dragon should have been able to enter unscathed. There was only one way that a dragon other than the Black King could land there and live to fly away: the Black King was gone.

To think that creature lived a thousand years... As a human, it was hard to comprehend, but the normal life span for a black dragon was a thousand years, and even then, it didn't truly die.

The biology of black dragons differed from other dragons. Instead of being born from an egg, a black dragon birthed an infant version of itself at the moment before its death. The parent passed on its name and memories to the infant before passing away.

My special mission was to capture the Black King; that is, to make it my familiar. To make a monster your familiar, you must make it submit to you—only possible if you are far stronger than the monster. After all, monsters won't submit unless they think they have no chance of winning. And to make a black dragon, an SS-rank monster, submit, we would need even greater strength—impossible strength, perhaps. Even a team of several brigades would surely fail.

But the period just after it reverted to infancy might be an exception. The dragon would need an entire year to grow back to its full strength. It was said that in the moments just after its birth, it was actually incredibly vulnerable. There was even a chance that it would think that the first creature it saw was its mother—egg-born dragons were known to imprint like that, and there was no telling whether asexual black dragons worked the same way. Uncertain, but worth a shot.

The people of the Náv Kingdom knew the black dragon as their guardian beast, but in reality, the creature was a vicious, calamity-class monster. Ordinary people only knew of the dragon from the coat of arms they saw across the kingdom and worshiped the beast in ignorance. The citizens had never learned of its brutal nature, likely because the monster rarely left its nest in Blackpeak Mountain.

In summary: the Black King, we believed, had lived out its thousand years and reverted to infancy. We could not waste the opportunity to capture it—it might be centuries before we got that chance again. I joined up with the Eleventh, the brigade in charge of protecting the north, and headed to Blackpeak Mountain the moment I received my mission.

The north was in chaos, having lost its supreme ruler. Monsters fought each other, seeking to become the new master of the land. I felt as though I'd been thrust back into times of war and chaos, watching local warrior-kings vie for territory and control.

After what felt like an eternity, we reached the depths of Blackpeak Mountain's caves and found...nothing. The only thing there was the massive, magnificent corpse of a black dragon, toppled onto its side. I could only assume that the infant black dragon's memories hadn't set in yet, and it left in a panic. Dragons hated sunlight by nature, so it would likely find a cave or a similarly dark place to roost.

Though I worried about the state of my brigade, I still spent the next half a year searching caves across the continent with the help of each region's managing brigade. No matter where I searched, I never found so much as a trace of the black dragon.

I'd just finished another fruitless, miserable cave search when a courier brought me news of a black dragon sighting near the royal castle in Starfall Forest. It had appeared, they said, from a hole in the sky that swirled with dark clouds, rain, and lightning. Multiple eyewitness testimonies backed the claim. The witnesses described the dragon as black, gorgeous, *sublime!* All were sure that it must be the dragon king.

I was ecstatic when I heard the news, but crestfallen as well. The prospect of laying eyes on the legendary black dragon excited me, but... it had grown more than I'd anticipated. It surely couldn't be captured now. The thought was crushing.

Carrying these conflicting feelings, I returned to the royal palace and reported to the captain. He thanked me for my efforts, but I felt nothing but shame at my failure.

Despite my exhaustion, I decided to pay a visit to my good old office. I hoped Gideon was holding down the fort well in my absence.

A bit apprehensive, I opened the door to my office...only to find two calamity-class monsters inside. I was so tired that the words slipped out of my mouth before I realized.

"Give me a break. I take a short leave and suddenly there are two calamity-class monsters in my office?"

For years, I'd been able to see a faint, smoky aura around people that told me how powerful they were. It seemed to factor in not just strength, but any abilities the person had, and it had never been wrong. Ever since I joined the Fourth Monster Tamer Knight Brigade, I trained my ability until I could read the auras of monsters as well. And at that moment, I was in the presence of two monstrous auras, the likes of which I'd never seen.

I couldn't help grimacing at the sight. My body stiffened, and a cold sweat prickled on the back of my neck. Without even realizing it, I took a step back.

One of the two auras belonged to a blue monster with its neck sticking out of a young knight's collar, but...what on earth was I supposed to do with *that*? The sheer pressure emitting from its body seemed impossible, as if its overwhelming aura was being squeezed into an undersized container.

I sighed. *If it wanted to, that thing could probably blow this entire building sky high... Dammit...*

I had a theory about the beast. I'd seen S-rank monsters more times than I could count, and their powers paled in comparison. Hell, their auras looked downright cute next to *this*. I didn't want to believe it, but this was probably an SS-rank monster. Add in our recent sighting in Starfall Forest, and it was obvious—this was almost certainly the black dragon I was looking for.

Ha...ha ha...damn it all! I'd spent half a year looking for a black dragon, and here it was...in my office.

I gazed at the black dragon, dark thoughts swirling in my mind. The beast leaped out of the young knight's collar and onto *its* shoulder.

The bluebird of happiness, I thought blearily. *Like the children's story. It ended with the main character returning home, sad that they couldn't find the bluebird, only to find it in their house. It's supposed to mean that happiness is closer than you think. Heh... the black dragon disguising itself as a bluebird makes a twisted kind of sense, like a sick joke meant only for me. The black dragon you've been looking for—that beast that brings death wherever it goes—was actually right here the whole time, waiting in the narrow space of your office where nobody can escape it! Ahh...a sick joke indeed. And the one responsible is surely the other monstrosity in the room.*

I clenched my fists until my knuckles went white, and I slowly turned my gaze to the other *monster*, the one I'd been avoiding even looking at. It wore a blue knight uniform and appeared to take the form of a girl, but...just what was *it*? Its aura was so vast that I couldn't even see its outline.

How the hell can the others stand being in the same room as this thing? The pressure is unbearable. I can't stop trembling. My ears... they won't stop ringing.

It made me jealous of anyone who *couldn't* see it! They probably only saw a young girl with a small, blue monster on her shoulder, but I knew the truth.

The fact that *it* was playing nonchalantly with the black dragon was a testament to how terrifying the *thing's* true power must have been.

What am I supposed to do in this situation? What can *I do? Are we already doomed? Is there no escaping our fate? This* thing *will surely torment us, humiliate us...* What could we expect from this creature but cruelty? It had carefully prepared this vile bluebird joke, after all.

I ran a hand through my hair with a trembling hand, trying to think of a solution to my predicament, when the monster in the shape of a young girl approached me with a smile.

A TALE OF THE SECRET SAINT

"It's a pleasure to meet you, Captain Quentin. My name's Fia Ruud, from the First Knight Brigade. Hee hee...you said there were two monsters, but actually one of them is a puppet I made!"

The *monstrosity* held out its left hand, encased in a misshapen bundle of cloth.

Is this a trap? I was afraid to say anything. Who knew what words might lead the creature to strike? At any moment, it might destroy me on a whim. Sweat dribbled down my back. My uniform clung to my skin; I'd arrived mere minutes ago and now it was positively drenched. *Is there a riddle hidden in the monster's words? Is it testing me?*

I found myself grasping for an answer, and for the first time, my life hung in the balance.

SIDE STORY
Fia, Healing Adventurers for a Good Cause!

I WATCHED FROM MY SEAT atop a comfortable rock as a party of adventurers made their way into the forest. It had already been two hours since I started my search, but I still hadn't found a suitable party.

There were two months left until the Knight Brigade admission exam. I'd spent the past month experimenting with my Great Saint powers, but there was only so much I could do alone. I'd practiced strengthening magic and equipment-enchanting magic over and over, but it was difficult to test how well I could heal injuries or status ailments—something I probably should have realized sooner.

That's why I came to this forest aimed at mid-level adventurers—not the one I'd gone to for my coming-of-age ceremony, to be clear—hoping to find injured people to practice on. I was looking for a party that looked likely to get hurt a lot while *also* being desperate enough to take in a complete stranger like me.

Yeah, I figured I'd be looking for a while...

I couldn't let anyone know I was a saint either, so the *best* option would be a party that was just passing through and would never see me again...but at the rate things were going, I felt like I'd be lucky to find *any* party.

Maybe I should try something else. No sooner had I thought that when a party of three men came into sight. All three were well built and wore imposing suits of armor, but two of them had blood dribbling down their foreheads.

Whoa...they're already injured, and they haven't even entered the forest? That's new. Wait, maybe this is exactly what I'm looking for!

Judging by the coat of arms on their armor, they were likely knights in a noble's employ. Knights had that whole chivalry thing going on, so I bet right then that they'd be more than willing to help a damsel in distress, even if it meant letting a teenage girl join a party of men.

I'm not gonna get a better chance. I called out to them, and all three turned around. They had incredibly annoyed looks on their faces the moment I entered their view.

"What is it, lass? You wouldn't be lost, would you? I'd hope not, at least not when you're only at the *entrance* of the forest."

I perked up at his words. Wearing this village girl dress that came down to my knees had done the trick. None of them thought I was from a knight family—he even called me "lass"!

I resisted the urge to grin and dabbed my eyes with a handkerchief, pretending to cry. "My cruel stepmother told me not to come home until I picked some herbs from the depths of the forest, but...I'm just a weak little girl, there's no way I could do it alone! Please, allow me to travel with you. I promise I won't—"

"Wh-what an awful stepmother! Don't worry, you can come with us!" The red-haired man in the group had looked suspicious at first, but his expression softened as he listened to my plea. It wasn't long before he was so overcome with emotion that he didn't even wait for me to finish.

"Wait, what?! I, uh, really? I wasn't even finished talking," I said, dropping all pretense in my surprise.

The green-haired man looked at me as though sizing me up. "Normally, we'd say no. But you clearly don't pose any threat to us. Besides, this guy here is reckless enough that he'll gladly fight till he kicks the bucket. Giving him someone to protect will keep him in line. Yes, definitely." The guy nodded at his own words. "Mh-hmm..."

These guys are kinda weird. Maybe I chose the wrong party after all?

I'd spent the month since I recovered my past life's memories testing what powers I could use, and I was pretty certain I had most of my protection spells. Barring any unforeseen circumstances, I wouldn't be in any danger as long as there was someone to attack...but teaming up with a suicidal fighter could be risky.

Maybe I shouldn't have called out to this party. But what kind of saint would I be if I left them out to dry now?

"All right," the redhead cried, "we're a team now, lass! If you have any problems during the trip, just speak up, ya hear?"

Ahh, it'd be kind of awkward to say anything now...but this red-haired guy is actually kind of nice. Maybe I chose the right party after all.

"The name's Red! I'm a swordsman, as you can see," said the red-haired man, pointing at himself. He looked like he was in his thirties, though I couldn't make out too many features through the blood dribbling down his forehead.

"This green-haired guy is Green. He's good with axes." Red pointed at the most well-mannered looking person in the group, a green-haired man who must've been in his mid-twenties... though he was bleeding from the forehead too, which made it a little hard to tell.

"And that pretentious guy with blue hair is Blue, a swordsman like me." Red pointed to Blue—he was standing apart from the group. He seemed like a taciturn man in his early twenties, and he was strikingly handsome...though it was hard to enjoy that when I remembered the other two guys with faces covered in blood.

Strange guys. Two bloody faces and one handsome...but I guess all that matters is whether they're strong? I grinned as I extended my hand for a handshake. *I better introduce myself too. Their whole aliases based off hair-color gimmick sounds kind of fun; I might as well join in!*

"Nice to meet you. My name's Midday Sparkling Scarlet, and

I'm a humble herb picker. You can just call me 'Sparkle Midday' for short!"

"Wait, your name's really, uh...Midday?" Red asked dubiously.

"For now it is, because it's midday, of course! My name changes depending on the time of day! Soon I'll be 'Sparkle Twilight', and when darkness falls? I become 'Sparkle Midnight'!"

"Sounds like a pain in the arse! What do people normally call you?!"

"Fia. Why?"

"Then that's that—you're 'Fia'!"

"Whaaaat?! No way, I want a cool alias too!" But it was too late. I'd let my real name slip. Everyone was all "Nice to meet you, Fia," and I had to shake their hands while *knowing* that I could've had a way cooler name. What an empty feeling...

W-well, whatever! I'm only here to test my saint powers, so it's not like I care or anything. Ugh. I couldn't even convince *myself* of that...

We made our way into the depths of the forest. Red led the party, followed by Green and me, with Blue bringing up the rear.

En route, Red suddenly turned around like he'd just remembered something. "Oh, right. I don't know jack about herbs. If you see anything you're looking for, just give me a holler. We'll wait for you to check."

That's awfully nice of him. "Thank you! How long were you three planning on staying in the forest?" I asked, eyeing their heavy-looking baggage. My older sister had already returned to her brigade, so I could get home a bit later than usual. Honestly, I could probably stay out for days on end. I doubted that any of the knights or squires at our estate would care enough to notice my absence.

"We're looking at something like, oh...a week to ten days? Depends on how long it takes to find that monster."

T-ten days?! I didn't bring anywhere near enough underwear! I'd only brought what I could fit inside my bag. Of course, a young lady couldn't let these men discover my dire underwear situation, so I played it cool. "Hmm! *Most* intriguing."

Underthings aside, I noticed that Red and Green were still bleeding from their foreheads. I didn't recognize the coat of arms on their armor, so...maybe they came from a distant country where constant bleeding was just kinda fine?

Green noticed me sneaking glances. "What's the matter?"

"Ah, no...uh...well, sorry if I'm being impolite, but not many people constantly bleed from their foreheads in this part of the world? I was wondering if you three were from some country where that's the norm."

Red burst out laughing. "That's hilarious! I ain't ever heard of such a country in my life!"

"R-really?! Um, then I'd rather people not give us weird looks. How about I patch you two up?" I brought two small cloths out of my bag and pressed a cloth against Green's forehead when I realized...

This isn't just any wound. This is a curse, and an old one at

that. It must be pretty strong to have lasted this long. I can't get the
bleeding to stop.

"Thanks," said Green with a smile, "but it's all right. Red and I have blood that just doesn't clot well." He held the cloth to his forehead.

"Is that so? I'm...sorry to hear that." I guess if they didn't want to talk about the curse, I wouldn't ask about it. But maybe there was a better way to approach this. "Actually, there's something I need to tell you three." I handed Red a cloth. "The truth is...I'm cursed."

"What?!" Red and Green exclaimed in unison.

"Yes. it's called the 'If you don't fight as a saint when you team up with adventurers, you won't get married until you're really old' curse."

The entire party gave me a look.

"And it gets worse! See, it came with the 'If your party disbands before reaching their destination, all your party members will have lady troubles for the rest of their lives' curse! I know, I know...it's a nightmare."

Red gave a weak chuckle. "C'mon! That's way too weird to be real. Besides, you're not a saint! Saints are all with the church. You wouldn't catch one traveling with adventurers in a hundred years!"

"You're right," I said. "I didn't have saint powers when I was checked at three and ten years old, so I'm not a saint. But when I got cursed, I gained the ability to temporarily use saint powers. Whew. Curses, man. They're really something. You gotta hate 'em, curses, like the one that I have."

More doubtful looks.

"I ain't ever heard of a curse giving you powers," said Red with a grimace, "but...all right. You're probably just messin' around, but the worst that could happen is that you use some saint powers. I don't see a downside to that." He folded his arms.

"We'll play along with your story," added Green with a grin, "but I wouldn't try it on anybody else."

Blue, a short distance away from the group, remained silent.

"Understood," I said with a smile. "Thank you for being so understanding."

Whoa, I can't believe I managed to convince them that I can use saint powers without being a saint! I'm almost too *good at this.*

The four of us continued deeper into the forest. The three seemed to know the way, plunging forward without hesitation. We encountered monsters many times, the first of which was a weak rabbit-like monster with a horn. It only took Red and Green a single swing to kill it.

"We'll be eatin' good tonight!" said Red as he shoved the monster into a bag.

The next monster we met was a foxlike creature with two tails, roughly the size of a large dog. I thought it'd put up a fight, but Red and Green's teamwork let them take it out without sustaining a single injury. As for Blue, he still hadn't even fought.

W-wow! Everyone's really strong. Maybe I chose the wrong party after all. I might not get a chance to even use my saint powers at this rate, I thought as I idly watched the two fight, getting increasingly bored.

We encountered a bird-type monster and a snake-type monster after that, both of which Red and Green beat like it was nothing.

Yeah, there's no point in me even being here...

Just as Red had claimed, dinner that night was good...and by good, I mean meat, meat, and more meat!

"Mmm! Delicious!" Nothing beat freshly caught meat, cooked on the spot over a crackling campfire. I grinned sloppily as I bit into the meat. *I really gotta do something to repay everybody.*

The one who did the cooking—in other words, made the fire and cooked the meat—was Blue. Red did the skinning, Green got water from the nearby river, and me? I just ate.

What do I do? I haven't done a thing! Surely I have some kind of special skill that'll help, right? I racked my brain, but I couldn't come up with anything. *Ugh, I'm totally useless!*

"Something wrong, Fia?" Red asked, noticing me freeze up mid-bite. "Was the meat burnt?" I looked to see both Green and Blue looking my way as well.

These three are so nice... They care so much about some shady village girl they only just met. "No, Blue's cooking is perfect. Super delicious! I was just thinking about how useless I've been..."

"C'mon, you're just a kid!" said Red. "When I was your age, I caused a whole bunch of trouble for the adults around me. That's just what a kid's job is—causing trouble for adults. You haven't even done *that* yet, heh! C'mon, get to work!" Red smiled and gave me a slap on the back.

Oww! Jeez, these guys really are *nice.* Even if my back throbbed a little—I guess Red didn't know his own strength—I could tell that he was a kind man. I was grateful I met these three from the bottom of my heart.

That was when Blue, who I hadn't heard speak a word yet, spoke up. "Fia, there's something I've been wanting to tell you since we first met."

"Y-yes, what is it?" I stood up straight and put my hands above my knees, sitting politely.

Blue glared at me. "I understand you have your reasons for coming to this forest. You've been keeping up with our fast pace without a single complaint, so I can tell you're serious, but—" He paused for a moment, and his glare turned scathing. "You shouldn't be joining an all-male party! Just because you're a child doesn't mean you're safe—there are people out there who would do terrible things, even to a child! Next time you have to join a party, make sure at least half of them are women! Understood?!"

"Yes, sir! I'll be more careful next time!"

Oh, wow. Blue is a nice person too, even if I'm already an adult. Actually, just what about me makes Red and Blue think I'm a child? I was a little hung up on that, but correcting Blue now would just earn me an even bigger scolding. I decided to keep my trap shut and just nodded.

We had resumed eating when Green spoke to me as he skewed another piece of meat. "You're a strange one. No normal person would want to team up with a bunch of intimidating men with blood dripping down their faces. What made you want to join us?"

"Hmm...well, I have my weird curse thing to consider, so I figured I should try joining the most problematic-looking group. See, a group like that wouldn't reject *me* for being shady, you know?" I answered honestly.

The three of them stopped eating.

I continued with a grin. "That's when you shady-looking three came strolling along. Heh heh, did you notice how the other parties at the forest entrance reacted when they saw you? All the girls took one look at you all and either fell on their backs or ran off with a shriek! Even I was surprised to see two men bleed from their foreheads, and this was before any of you guys set foot in the forest!"

Green let out a huge sigh. "You're really something else, Fia," he said, staring into the fire. "The three of us...we come from well-to-do families. But because of our abnormal forehead bleeding, people fear us. They avoid us like the plague. As a matter of fact, I can't remember the last time I had a proper conversation with a girl like you. You're an odd one, just talking to us like it's nothing."

He seemed to have a lot on his mind. I had to admit it—normally I'd never want to associate with someone who constantly bled from their forehead. But it seemed silly to worry about it now that I knew how kind they were.

I continued to stuff my cheeks when I noticed Red acting strangely. He hesitated for a moment, carefully picking his words. Finally, he spoke. "Fia, there's something we've been withholding from you. The three of us came to this forest to hunt down the Twin-Headed Turtle."

"The Twin-Headed Turtle?"

The three of them nodded gravely.

I recalled the memories of my past life. *Let's see...the Twin-Headed Turtle should be a powerful monster native only to the Náv Kingdom, so...wait! A powerful monster? This is my chance! Finally, I can make myself useful!*

I turned to face the three and leaped to my feet.

"Figures," said Red sadly. "We'll take you back to the forest entrance tomor—"

"Finally, my chance to shine!" I said, cutting him off—didn't want him to get the wrong idea, after all! "You can count on me to help you take down the Twin-Headed Turtle!"

"Um..." Red blinked a few times, not comprehending my words. "What?!"

Brimming with confidence, I grinned. "I have my curse to worry about, remember? I have the 'If you don't fight as a saint when you team up with adventurers, you won't get married until you're really old' curse! I'm not about to be single until I'm old, thank you very much!"

Red sighed for some reason.

Green spoke up, sounding exhausted. "Do as you like. Just talking with you is wearing me out. I knew you weren't normal when you weren't afraid of us, but you're really not afraid of a Twin-Headed Turtle? I guess you're also cursed with being damn daft."

"Wha—?! Hey, rude! Besides, you three aren't scary at all! You're good people, and you're all really nice and brave! You make a little bleeding seem like nothing!" There we go! Would a daft person say *that?* But... "Huh? Is something wrong?"

Their faces had flushed beet red. "Y-you really *are*! Saying something like that so bluntly with a straight face? C'mon!" Red bellowed, his face bright as a cherry.

"Th-that surprised me..." Green mumbled. "I've never been complimented before in my life, and so directly? I...don't know what to say."

Blue's face was scarlet from ear to ear as he thrust a piece of meat into my mouth. "Just be quiet and eat!"

"Nh, okah. Fank yho bery mush." *Are these grown men actually super shy? Aww, isn't that sweet?*

The three of them kept on feeding me delicious meat, and I went to sleep that night with a full belly.

We continued even deeper into the forest the next day. The Twin-Headed Turtle was said to make its home upstream, so we traveled along the river. Every now and then a monster appeared, but Red and Green only fought the ones that attacked us—we already had enough food stored. The two of them remained unscathed.

"Something wrong?" Green asked, noticing my gaze. We'd just stopped for a short break.

"Nothing, I was just admiring how strong you are," I answered honestly.

Green made a strange *"Gah!"* sound and collapsed to his knees.

"G-Green, you fool!" Red scolded. "Did you forget how destructive this girl can be?! You've got to be careful talking to her!"

"Y-you're right! How could I be so foolish?! To think a single blow would deal this much damage. I shouldn't have let my guard down..."

I looked down at the two of them. "You two really are strong, though. How can you fight so much without getting hurt once?"

"S-stop that!" Red exclaimed. "Not a word more!"

Green shook his head. "What are you even talking about? Nobody wants to get hurt in a fight. It's not like healing potions can heal our wounds on the spot."

"Oh, that makes sense! So that kind of fighting style was adopted to make up for the lack of saints. Makes sense. So I imagine you guys don't often have saints as backup, then?"

Green gave me an odd look. "You kidding me? There isn't a snowball's chance in hell that we'd fight alongside a saint. They only work with royalty and nobility; they'd never work with adventurers!"

"Gotcha. So it's the same in the Arteaga Empire?"

The three's eyes went wide. Red and Green stood up wordlessly, and Blue moved a step closer to me.

H-huh? What's going on? Did I say something rude?

Red's expression was stiff. "How do you know we're from Arteaga?"

"Huh? I heard you speaking Arteagian in your sleep last night, so I guessed. Was I wrong?" *I wasn't a princess in my last life for nothin'! I have all the important languages down!*

They were totally silent.

"There's also that coat of arms on your armors. It took me a while to recognize it, but that's the Goddess of Creation, right? The one the Arteaga Empire worships?" Or at least that's what my previous life knew. "But, um, if I was wrong and somehow made you uncomfortable, I'm sorry..."

Green seemed to lose his energy mid-way through my explanation and sat down again. "You're kidding me. I can't believe that there's someone all the way out in the sticks who can understand Arteagian!"

"We chose this backwater place so nobody would find us out, and yet...here we are. Fia, is one of your parents or grandparents from the Empire? Damn, I hadn't considered that; not a lot of people start new lives outside the Empire." Red slumped down before looking over at me. "Oh, don't worry—we're not outlaws or anything. We're not going to do anything to you now that you know, but I'd appreciate it if you didn't tell anyone where we're from."

I couldn't help giggling. There was something silly about a grown, muscular man asking for a favor. "Of course! I'll take it to the grave!"

"Good, good," Green said, ruffling my hair messily. "Did you catch that, Blue? She'll keep our secret, so you better not lay a hand on her."

"Hmm."

"Blue, that's not an answer!"

"Understood, Brother," he said reluctantly.

"Whoa, don't just *say* that!" Green said in a panicked voice.

Blue stared back defiantly. "What's it matter at this point?"

Ignoring the two, Red set down his baggage. "Ahh, I'm pooped. How 'bout a lunch break?" He pointed at Green and Blue with a sigh. "Those two idiots are my little brothers. Green's the second oldest. Blue's the third. We've also got a little sister back home."

"O-oh. Um, I also have three siblings. Two older brothers and an older sister." We had something in common after all!

"Huh. What a coincidence," said Red. The other two looked over too, interested.

On Red's suggestion, we began preparing for lunch. For some reason, the usually distant Blue invited me to fetch water with him. I accepted, ecstatic that he was opening up to me.

He seemed like a completely different person as we walked, friendly and talkative. "You're quite knowledgeable. Even if you did have family from the Empire, I'm still surprised that someone from the Náv Kingdom knew Arteagian and the Goddess' coat of arms. Tell me, Fia, why do you think the three of us came here?"

"Huh? To hunt the Twin-Headed Turtle like you guys said, right? The Twin-Headed Turtle can only be found in Náv, so you'd have to come all this way to hunt it."

"Ha! So you're even knowledgeable about monsters. The Náv Kingdom must be really something if even a common villager knows this much. Or maybe you're just special?"

"You're...really friendly all of the sudden. Why the change?" I asked, surprised.

"Ah, that. I'm actually fairly talkative most of the time—maybe *too* talkative. But I didn't want to let our cover slip by accident, so I kept my distance and clammed up. Seeing as you already know our big secret, and Green made me promise not to do anything to you, I suppose there's no point in me being quiet anymore."

"I see. You three really are kind. Is it because the Arteaga Empire worships the Goddess that you're all such gentlemen?" I said, turning around with a smile...only to find Blue hanging his head and biting his lip. "B-Blue?"

He met my eyes and forced a smile. "Does the Goddess really exist, I wonder?" With that, he took the water I'd scooped up and quickly made his way back.

Lunch was lively. I got the impression that the brothers were trying to keep things light; Blue talked and laughed a lot.

Whenever I stopped eating to laugh at one of Blue's jokes, Red took a piece of meat and stuck it in my mouth. "You ain't growing right! You need to eat more meat! Meat, meat!"

"Nh, yesh!" I said through a mouthful.

Blue laughed as I tried my hardest to chew the massive mouthful. "Oh man, you look like a small animal. Yeah, I...I wonder if that's what she'd be like..."

Hm? What's that mean? I looked up at Blue.

Blue gave me a pained smile as he continued. "Our little sister's in something of a Sleeping Beauty situation, you see."

"Blue!" Red warned.

Oh right, they mentioned they have a sister back home. Do they call her Sleeping Beauty because she sleeps a lot?

Blue looked directly at Red. "What's the point in hiding anything now, Brother? Fia...the children of our bloodline are sometimes born cursed. My brothers were cursed to bleed forever, and my sister was cursed to sleep forever." He laughed mirthlessly. "Just like a certain fairy tale, don't you think?"

"Huh?! You mean...she's been asleep since she was born?" I blurted. *But if she's close to Blue's age or something, she'd be in her twenties. You're telling me she's been sleeping for over twenty years? And...if the curse starts at birth, then Red and Green have been bleeding for at least twenty-five, thirty years! That's terrible!*

Blue looked down and grimaced. "I wasn't breathing when I was born. They expected me to die. That's why the curse didn't fall on me, I suppose. I wasn't even worth the effort."

"Blue!" This time Green yelled to warn his brother.

Blue ignored him and continued on. "In our family, those born cursed are considered sinners. It's said that our punishments are equal to our sins. We're told, too, that if we repent and do good deeds, the Goddess of Creation will remove our curse and make us the finest statesmen around. That's why my brothers have been working hard to do good deeds, as have I in my sleeping sister's place. But...the curses still remain." He laughed bitterly. "There is no Goddess in our empire. The curses will never be removed..."

"Blue!" Red lunged forth and gripped his brother's collar. "Don't speak ill of the Goddess or you'll be cursed!"

"You know I won't! The Goddess doesn't exist! If she did, your curses would've been removed a long time ago! She wouldn't just stand by as you two *die*!"

"Blue!" Red socked his brother in the face to try and quiet him.

Blue fell to the ground and looked up at Red with disdain. I stood up and—not knowing what else to do—jumped between them. "W-w-wait! I-I don't think your curses are lethal, so how about we calm down?"

Blue sat on the ground and wiped the blood off the cut on his lip. "You're right, Fia. The *curse* isn't going to kill my brothers, no. They'll be murdered at the hands of a human. Our father will soon choose his heir. The oldest son, Red, would normally be the heir... but father won't dare as long as he suffers this curse!" He spat his words. "We have countless siblings born to different mothers who can become heir. When they do—and they *will*!—the three of us will be banished from our home and likely killed by assassins. We're a risk to our stepsiblings, you see." Sitting on the ground, Blue held his head in his hands.

He shook his head. "But...*ha!* Why am I even telling you this? Am I trying to repent? Am I confessing my failures to you in place of my sister? It's your hair, perhaps. It's the same as hers. I'm sorry...I'm sorry I couldn't protect you." Blue hid his face with trembling hands.

I didn't know what to say. "Blue..."

Right then, Green—who'd been watching without a word—came up behind Blue and knocked him on the back of his head. "You're crying your heart out to a kid? Act your age!" He smiled at me. "Sorry about that. Blue gets depressed easily. Our story's not all doom and gloom; our country's best diviner told us that Red and I would have our curse removed if we killed a Twin-Headed Turtle. And if we cook the Twin-Headed Turtle's left foreleg and feed it to our sister, her curse will be removed too! Two birds with one stone, eh?"

"Hmph!" Blue turned away in a huff. "You know well that the diviner was a sham hired by our stepbrother! Utter nonsense, all of it!"

"Yeah, well, not like we have much choice but to try after they did that whole divining performance in front of everyone. Sure, maybe it's a plot to get us killed by a giant turtle so they don't need to dirty their own hands, but wouldn't it be hilarious if we actually came back with the Twin-Headed Turtle's left foreleg?"

"Assuming we come back alive," Blue said sourly.

Green wore a troubled smile. "Yeah. Uh, Blue? When the time comes—"

"How dare you?! I won't run away. What would be left of me if I did? I'd be someone who abandoned his sister, his brothers, his pride! Only regret would remain until the day I died!"

"Yeah...okay. Forget I said anything." Green shook his head and offered me a thin smile. "Sorry you had to get involved in our mess. The diviner said that Red and I have to defeat the Twin-Headed Turtle by ourselves. If something happens to us, run away with Blue. He'll keep you safe."

I shook my head. "No. When you let me join the party, you said that Red is so reckless, 'he'll gladly fight till he kicks the bucket.' You want me to keep him in line? I intend to. I'm gonna keep Red *and* you alive!"

"Fia—"

"Besides, I can help you all with the saint powers I got from my curse!"

Green's face finally brightened up. He chuckled. "I forgot. I'm sure we'll be all right as long as we believe we have a saint on our side."

I returned his smile with a bright grin of my own.

The three were back to normal the next morning. I was worried that things would be sour between them after yesterday's events, but it turned out fine. Perhaps they were the sort who forgot everything after a good night's sleep, or perhaps they were just playing it cool so they didn't worry me. Whatever the reason, they were just as cheerful as before.

"We've come quite a way upstream. Let's hope for a super-small baby Twin-Headed Turtle, yeah," I joked, grinning broadly.

"*Pssh*, set your sights higher!" Green retorted. We shared a laugh and continued onward.

Right after lunch, when we were gearing up to move again, Blue went silent. I was concerned he was mulling over something again like last night when, suddenly, he stood up. Through shallow breaths, he said, "It's here."

"Hmph."

"I see..."

Red and Green showed no surprise, perhaps already expecting Blue's words.

Green looked at me and offered a smile. "Blue's got a knack for attack magic, especially detection stuff." He crouched down to my eye level. "Sorry we couldn't find those herbs you were after, but...thanks for coming with us. I got to feel what it might be like to go on an adventure with my little sister."

I was about to say something, but Red beat me to it. "You got pluck, Fia. Not just anybody's got the guts to stick around three shady guys and laugh the whole way. Thanks."

The two turned towards Blue and grinned. They spoke almost in unison—

"Blue, we'll show you how your brothers fight!" said Red.

"We were lucky to have a little brother like you!" said Green.

A sudden deafening splash drowned out the end of what they said. I turned, and there it was surfacing from the river—a giant Twin-Headed Turtle. We must've intruded on its territory, because it looked *mad*. Blue and I retreated to stay out of the way.

A Twin-Headed Turtle—a troublesome monster capable of movement on land and water. Its body was around five meters in length, with a spiky shell on its back for protection. Its two heads attacked as one, and its sharp teeth could easily crush bone. No way could Red and Green handle something like this.

The monster moved out of the water with great momentum, stopping a short five meters before Red and Green. It ground its teeth together, making a loud, threatening noise. It must have been terrifying up close, but the two showed no fear as they readied their weapons.

Green moved first.

"Hyaaah!" He sprung forward with a leap, swinging his axe down on the monster's shell. His axe deftly avoided the spikes and struck the shell cleanly—only to rebound without leaving a dent. "Damn!"

Green recovered and swung down at the monster's foreleg... just as its right head turned towards him with its mouth wide open. He immediately abandoned the attack and leapt back diagonally...but he was a moment too late. A sickening sound resounded as its jaws snapped shut. Blood sprayed everywhere.

A chunk of flesh was missing from Green's shoulder...and yet he still stood, gritting his teeth.

Red swung his sword horizontally at the right head as it chewed Green's flesh. This time, however, the monster's left head reacted, positioning its mouth to bite Red. Red ducked to dodge, but the head followed him, enveloping Red's left elbow with its mouth. Green reacted instantly, his axe gashing one of the left head's eyes.

"Got 'em!" His axe landed true, crushing one of the monster's eyes. But his success was short-lived. The monster swung its body in a half circle and bashed both of them with its immense tail, knocking them several meters into the air. The two began to descend...and waiting for them below was a pair of gaping jaws.

They tried to twist their bodies midair to dodge but couldn't manage it—not fully. Red lost everything below his right elbow, and Green his right ear. Blood splattered in all directions. The Twin-Headed Turtle unleashed a triumphant roar.

"Blue!" I yelled, feeling the monster's roar reverberate through my body. But Blue didn't respond in the slightest. He dug his teeth into his lip. Blood trickled down his chin. He clenched his fists, but he showed no sign that he even heard my voice. He only watched, unblinking, as his brothers fought. His legs trembled and his feet dug into the earth, but he made no attempt to move.

"Blue! We need to help them!" I couldn't sit still any longer. I could understand him not interfering because he trusted the strength of his brothers, but that wasn't it, not now. At that moment, Blue was fully prepared to watch his brothers die just to preserve their honor in carrying out some diviner's nonsensical words.

If Blue didn't fight now, he'd regret it—just as he'd said last night. "What's the point of it all if they die?!" I shouted, raising my voice to its limit. Blue finally reacted, looking at me with a hint of surprise. There we go. I had to get through to him. "The Goddess can't do anything for them if they're already gone! What's more important, your brothers or their curse?!"

"Fia...I..."

"The monster has two heads! It can only attack two people at once! They *need* your help, Blue!"

Life returned to Blue's eyes. Power swelled in his body. His eyes narrowed with long-overdue determination, but he hesitated once more. "But, Fia...if I join them and die, who will get you back safely?"

My heart ached. Finally I understood the true reason Red and Green had allowed me to join their party—I was to be the fetters holding their little brother back. I was to be the thing that kept him alive.

Such doting older brothers...and such a chivalrous younger brother. I smiled at Blue. "I'll be okay. Go help your brothers! Besides, if I run away, my curse will kick in and I won't get married until I'm a granny!"

Blue's doubts seemed to finally clear. He ran forward, drawing his blade and shouting. "Allow me to join you, my brothers! And I beg of you, overlook the carelessness of your foolish younger brother!"

Wow. Just how fancy do you have to be to speak so formally at a time like this? I wondered.

"Allow me to provide my assistance as a saint!" I cried. "I shall boost your strength to match the foul beast's, and I swear that I shall heal your injuries as they come! Go forth, knights, for Goddess and Empire!" (Okay, I could see why they liked talking like this.)

I began casting healing magic. Instantly, Red's elbow and arm and Green's shoulder and ear began to regenerate.

"Huh?" The two looked flabbergasted, standing stock-still in the middle of the battle. They stared blankly at their healed bodies as though their brains had come to a standstill.

Turtle! We still have a big turtle to fight! The two slowly looked back at me. "Focus, you two!" I snapped, frowning. "The fight's not over!"

They regained their senses and turned back to the monster. I extended my right hand, palm first, and cast strengthening magic. "Invigorate: Attack ×2; Speed ×2!" Then I extended my left hand towards the Twin-Headed Turtle and cast weakening magic. "Enfeeble: Earth Attribute −30%!"

All right...now the three of them should be strong enough to handle it!

Taking care not to overdo my spells, I assisted them with my saint powers. The three *should* believe I could conditionally use saint powers due to a curse, but I was still a little worried they'd think I was a real saint—that's why I stuck to abilities that an average saint might use.

I'd heard that saints are weaker now than they were in my previous life, but this much should be okay...right?

For some reason, the three looked back at me with surprise the moment I cast my strengthening magic. But there was no time to explain. "Just go for it, guys! It'll be an easy win!"

Even from a distance, I could see the three gulp nervously. They slowly turned back to the Twin-Headed Turtle and readied their weapons.

Sure enough, the brothers had the fight in the bag. They fought in perfect sync, likely because they'd been training together from a young age. Two of them distracted the heads, and the remaining brother took the opportunity to strike. Once, twice, three times...they repeated the pattern again and again. The difference in strength between them and the monster was almost hilarious—each sword swing pierced deep, and each axe strike removed chunks. Any attack the monster *did* manage to land was healed at once. It didn't take long at all for the finishing blow to be dealt, and rather anticlimactically. Red lopped off the left head, and shortly after, Green lopped off the right. With the monster now motionless, Blue cut off its left foreleg.

"Amazing! The three of you alone defeated the Twin-Headed Turtle, and in such a short time too!" I congratulated them, but they didn't respond.

They simply stood there, breathing heavily as they stared at the body of the monster. I had to wonder if they realized it was over.

Maybe they're still worked up and need some time to cool off? Yeah, that's gotta be it. They've been suffering with their curses their whole lives, right? This moment must mean a lot to them.

Deciding to let them bask in the moment, I set forth to fulfill my own task—collecting herbs. Originally, collecting herbs was just a story I fabricated to let me travel with them, but now I was doing it for real. Kinda cracked me up, honestly. *Heh heh...who would've thought?*

I took a vial I brought and filled it with river water and then added some moss stuck to the back of the Twin-Headed Turtle. I paused for a moment before scraping off some skin from the monster's left foreleg—held by Blue now—and adding it in. That last bit wasn't *really* needed, but I did it for their sake. I closed the vial and poured my magic in—not much, though. The necessary elements were already assembled, after all.

I put the vial in Red's hand and wrapped his fingers around it. "A sip of this potion should wake your sister up." He just looked at me absently.

I suspected that the "curse" applied to their sister was really the sleep status ailment. The effect must've been strong to persist for all these years, but I was sure I could cure it. After all, the one who'd afflicted their sister was likely the same person who'd afflicted the two brothers themselves...and their status ailments were something I could easily cure.

Their "curse" wasn't from the Goddess, but from a human being.

Perhaps the mother of their stepsiblings did this to them, or even a blood relative. Whoever it was, I was sure that they'd afflicted the siblings under the guise of a curse in an attempt to usurp the siblings' position as heir.

I hesitated, unsure whether I should tell them the truth—that somebody close to them was responsible for this "curse"—but one look at their faces told me all I needed to know.

Ah...so you three already knew, huh? You're all splendid adults who can look reality in the eye and see the truth of your own lives! Yep, no need for me to say anything at all!

"May I remove your curse, Red?" I asked, smiling weakly. I wasn't sure whether I should remove his curse when we'd first met—I hadn't known the first thing about him, after all. But now I was certain that the affliction had to go.

Red nodded wordlessly.

I smiled again. "I'll remove it now, so would you mind bending down?"

He let out a small gasp of surprise and hurriedly dropped to a knee. His eyes were awfully serious.

"Thou Knight Red, I shall now remove thy curse!" I placed my hand on his forehead and cast status ailment recovery magic. Light shimmered from my fingers and into his body. For the first time in the thirty years of his life, the bleeding that had plagued him came to an end...in the blink of an eye. I asked Green and repeated the same process, curing him as well.

Even after I finished, the three still wore vacant looks on their faces, Red and Green on one knee and Blue standing stock-still.

H-huh? Is something wrong? I shot them a worried look. "Um, I'm done now. Maybe we should start heading back?"

The three of them went totally stiff. "Yes, ma'am!"

They didn't say another word. It was like their tongues had been tied. In fact, they wouldn't even look me in the eye. Wordlessly, they rushed to pack up, loaded up their baggage, and started the journey home. It took us two days to reach the edge of the forest.

The three treated me cordially along the way, though they didn't let me hold my own bag for some reason, but they kept those same dim, blank looks on their faces and only spoke when absolutely necessary.

Midway through our trip back, I couldn't take it anymore. I had to come clean. "Um, actually...the part about my stepmother bullying me? That was a lie."

In response, I only got a curt "Understood."

The lie had been weighing on my mind ever since the three told me the truth about their sister, but they just accepted it like it was nothing. Thinking now was a good chance, I added, "My curse was also removed, so I can't use that saint power anymore. Do you think you three could keep the whole thing secret?"

I got the same curt answer: "Understood."

We eventually reached the edge of the forest. "Thank you very much for allowing me to accompany you three."

That was when the three dropped to a knee, surprising me, and chanted in unison:

"We thank thee, O almighty Goddess of Creation!"

Whuh?

"Forgive our foolish selves for lacking the piety to recognize your divine will," said Red in a mind-numbingly polite tone.

"We are humbled that You should grace us with Your divine incarnation, and honored to receive Your favor!"

"Um...come again?"

"We only ask that You might give our lowly selves a few words of guidance, so that Your sheep shall not stray from the path of the righteous!" said Green.

"We beg thee, O Goddess!" Blue added, just as nonsensically.

"What?" I was at a total loss. The three of them stared back at me, earnest and sincere. "Um, uhh..."

What are they even doing? Uh. When we first met, they introduced themselves with aliases...so maybe this is another strange adventurer custom? Or maybe Arteagians do stuff like this all the time?

Deciding it'd be tasteless not to play along, I racked my brain for something appropriate to say. *Let's see...they mentioned Red was going to be the heir of his family if their curses were removed, right?*

I made the softest expression I could and said, "Thou shall guide those under you righteously. I well know that the power and will to do so resides in thee, my children."

Seeing them still wear their stiff expressions, I got the urge to joke around a little. I tapped them on each of their shoulders. "I have just given you the power to forge a new path. So, you know. Get to it."

But the three of them didn't so much as grin at my joke, instead bowing their heads deeply as though in deep reverence.

It had been five days since I parted from the brothers and returned home. Despite being gone for so long, the knights of my family's domain didn't scold me or anything! I was gone for so long, and *still* they didn't even care!

Oh well. I enjoyed my adventure with the three brothers, but looking back on it, I hadn't gotten to test my saint powers very much.

So I promptly returned to the tried-and-true method of self-testing my abilities...

Months later, the Arteaga Empire—one of two large, powerful countries sharing the continent—crowned a new emperor. The one to rise to the throne was the previous emperor's eldest son, inheritor of the long and noble bloodline of the late Queen.

He knew no love, born cursed and denied any right to the throne...until he received the Goddess of Creation's blessing, which removed the curse from his body.

The new emperor, named after a red gem, stepped forth to address his people with his similarly named two younger brothers and one younger sister behind him.

"I have met the Goddess of Creation, and she has given me a great role and the power to fulfill it! I swear to serve the Goddess and guide this country and its people to peace and prosperity!"

Arteaga—the empire that worshiped the Goddess—greeted its new emperor with fervent cheers. But the day that its new emperor and his younger brothers would reunite with a certain young knight would not come for some time...

Saviz, Captain of the Knight Brigades

Together with the Winds of the Beginning

TWO REDS OVERLAPPED and seemed, to me, the same—the red of our flag billowing in the wind and the red of her hair. They were one. One and the same.

I happened to come across Fia—and her bright red hair—in the hallway one day. Upon noticing me, she moved to the edge of the hallway and bowed. Normally I would give a quick nod and pass by, but for reasons unknown to me, I found myself stopping before her.

She raised her head and looked at me curiously. I looked into those golden eyes and ordered her to follow me on the spot, acting on sheer impulse. My guards betrayed surprise for a moment, seeing me act out of character, but they soon returned to their stony-faced selves as Fia followed me upstairs.

We arrived at a balcony attached to the highest floor of the castle. It was unusually wide, large enough to fit Fia and a dozen of my guards.

"Whoa..." Fia looked down from the balcony, marveling. All of the kingdom could be seen from this spot. The multicolored rooftops sparkled as they reflected the sunlight, no doubt stunningly beautiful to her. Beneath every roof lived a citizen living a bright and beautiful life.

"Gorgeous, is it not?" I muttered to no one in particular. "This is the Náv Kingdom. This is the land I must protect."

Fia turned around, smiling from ear to ear. "What a coincidence!" she said energetically. "I was just thinking about how I wanted to protect this sight too!"

I frowned a bit. Perhaps it was my intuition as a leader, but I got the impression that I was missing something. I tried to follow her train of thought and grasp that missing piece when I was interrupted by a gust of wind.

"Whoa!" she exclaimed, trying to keep her tousled hair from flying everywhere. Past her, a line of flags hung from the balcony. The design of our proud Náv Kingdom's flag had a black dragon centered on an all red base. Fia's hair, however, seemed to fade into the red of the flag behind her...

"Your hair. It matches the flag," I said, my thoughts slipping past my mouth. Fia looked back at me quizzically.

"Hm? I guess? Red has many different shades though, so it's not *exactly* the same."

The red of our flag came from the Red of the Great Saint, a shade I'd believed to be unique to the Great Saint—that was, until now.

I didn't reply, checking the colors against each other again.

They...looked one and the same.

Originally, the flag of the Náv Kingdom was white and blue. But three hundred years ago, it was completely changed by the knight brigade captain of the time to match the Great Saint's red hair.

It was a well-known fact that the Red of the Great Saint was uniquely difficult to reproduce. It was said that dye craftsmen were given the challenge of their life when the flag was changed three hundred years ago. They all tried to reproduce the color but to no avail. Only one craftsman managed to make it, and only through a stroke of luck. Since then, the secret to reproducing the Red of the Great Saint was closely guarded, known only to a single line of dye makers. All national flags were dyed by that one workshop alone.

And yet that same rare, nearly unreproducible color was before me now.

"They are the same shade," I said.

"Oh really? Must be a really common shade, then," she replied with a smile, blissfully unaware.

That color was *never* passed down through family lines. It had been lost with the Great Saint. I remembered looking at a portrait of her when I was young and feeling utter divinity from the striking color. It was said to never appear naturally, and yet...

"Common?" I snapped reflexively. "Have you any idea how much a noblewoman would give to have hair that color?" At times, Fia was oddly ignorant about such commonly known things.

Sometimes nature did bring forth miraculous coincidences. Perhaps this girl, without an ounce of saint power, was one such coincidence. *But to have the same golden eyes as the Great Saint too?*

"It's unfortunate you don't have any saint power," I said. "Demonstrate just a little and you would be *worshiped*."

Fia looked confused for a moment. Then, with a carefully blank face, she nodded. "But of course, sir."

Obviously, she had no idea what I meant.

Don't nod along if you don't understand! I grumbled to myself.

Still, I stifled my weary sigh and beckoned Fia back into the room. "Sorry for making you come with me all of a sudden. I just happened to think that your hair and our kingdom's flag looked similar, and I wished to compare them."

"Hee hee! So even the great captain does childish things every now and then," she replied with a strange smile. She turned on her heel and made her way for the stairs. I noticed that the bodyguards were looking at her differently than they had before.

You're the only one who doesn't understand the significance of that color. Or perhaps there are more people in the world than I thought who have hair of such a striking color, but...no, I doubt it.

The Great Saint was once a princess of the royal family. Although she surely had blood relatives within the aristocracy, none ever had that same red.

Was this really just some miraculous coincidence?

"Don't go dyeing your hair, Fia," I said, worried about the ignorance she showed.

She smiled back at me. "Yes, sir! I've had this color my whole life, actually, and I like it quite a lot!"

"Is that so? Some people's hair color changes in childhood, but you...you've kept the same color?"

"Ah...hm. I guess so?" she replied vaguely.

I brought Fia back to where we'd met earlier, and she bowed to me. "Thank you for showing me that wonderful sight! I'll work my hardest today! Farewell!"

She's a lively one, all right. It wouldn't be bad to have more people like her in Náv.

I turned away and began walking to my next appointment.

A Tale of the
Secret Saint

Afterword

NICE TO MEET YOU. I'm the author, Touya. Thank you for reading this little story of mine, originally published as a web novel before being adapted into a book.

I initially started writing because I had too much unused paid vacation piled up. I'm actually an office worker, and I'd only used two hours of my paid vacation the previous year. Let me repeat that: I used *two hours* of a whole year's worth of vacation. I must be built pretty sturdy, because I didn't need sick leave once. Anyway, my boss found out and suggested I take some time off.

"Take a vacation, for goodness' sake! I better not see you in the office for a while! Gah, people will think I'm a slave driver if they see the records!"

So, on the last possible month, I traded in my paid vacation and took five days off.

Wh-what?! Five days off out of the blue?! What am I going to do?!—that was my immediate reaction. *All right, I'll go watch a movie, listen to music, read a book, eat some tasty things...*

I did all the things I normally wanted to do but got tired of it all after only *two* days.

What am I going to do for the last three days...? I know! I'll do something I don't usually do but want to try, like...writing a book...?

And so, entirely on impulse, I decided to write a book online.

When I first started writing, I thought I'd go with being as inoffensive and uncriticizable as possible. Oh, how boring I was... I quickly figured out that there was nothing you could do to keep your writing from being criticized. There was one thing I could control, though. People who abandoned works halfway got an awful lot of criticism, so I told myself I'd write a short novel with a clear end.

That way, readers would go, "Oh? Hey, this writer actually finished something. Guess I'll read their next work now that I know they won't ditch." Also, there was only so much I could do in three days...

But, to my surprise, more people liked it than I expected. Some even left comments behind.

Oh, jeez! O-oh, all right, maybe I'll write a little more...?

Even more people started reading. They said that they'd like to read the continuation and had bookmarked my work. Eventually, a publisher contacted me.

I-I need 120,000 characters to make a book? O-okay, understood!

Of course, I didn't know restraint, and before long my writing wouldn't fit into a single book. Looking back on it, I don't even know how I intended to finish this story as a short novel in the first place!

Oh...right, oops! I haven't talked about the book itself yet. Well...you know how not everyone picks up on certain things when they read between the lines? I think that talking about the book here might spoil some surprises for some readers. There are also the people who read the afterword *before* the book to think about too. In other words...we'll skip talking about the book! (Touya avoids responsibility yet again!)

The illustrator of the book is chibi. Allow me to share a little story from way back when. They were asking me if I had any preferences for an illustrator.

"I want someone who can draw handsome men!" I asserted.

"Let's see here...so you want someone who can draw cute female characters but *also* cool male characters. And monsters too, considering the dragon. In other words, you prefer an illustrator who can...draw well. Is that correct?" the editor-in-chief replied.

H-huh? Did I really say all that? Wow, I sound really demanding. Should I pull back and say I don't need all that? Mmm...but I really do want nice art!

Everyone, there comes a time in our lives where we have to make a stand.

"Y-yes, please!" I replied.

And thus, with the help of the talented editor-in-chief, chibi appeared like magic.

I could explain how amazing chibi's art is, but a picture is worth a thousand words and you already have this book! But I *do* want to mention how amazing the illustration on the first page turned out to be even when all the information I gave was:

Fia × Captain. If possible, please add flags fluttering in the back (black dragon on a red background).

Truly a testament to their skill! It was so good, I couldn't help writing a short story about it. Those who bought the first print edition of the book will find the short story sandwiched between the pages. Please take a long, hard look at the picture I mentioned before you read.

I'd like to end by thanking those who helped make this book a reality: the early readers who read and helped my work get noticed, the editors who advised me and helped make my writing clearer, chibi, who gave life to my characters, and all the people working behind the scenes to get this book into the readers' hands. This book could only be made thanks to all of them. I'd like to thank Earth Star Novels as well, of course, for publishing this book.

And I'd like to thank all the readers who picked it up.

Together, we made a truly wonderful book. Thank you.

Let your imagination take flight with Seven Seas' light novel imprint: Airship

Discover your next great read at
www.airshipnovels.com

Experience all that SEVEN SEAS has to offer!

My Alcoholic ESCAPE FROM REALITY
From the Bestselling Author of My Lesbian Experience with Loneliness, My Solo Exchange Diary
Story and Art by Nagata Kabi

SCHOOL ZONE GIRLS
STORY & ART: NINKYAU

Ride your Wave
The Manga
Manga by MACHI KIACHI
2019 RIDE YOUR WAVE FILM PARTNERS

ROLL OVER AND DIE
I Will Fight for an Ordinary Life with My Love and Cursed Sword!

MUSCLES ARE BETTER THAN MAGIC!
DORANEKO
RELUGI

BEFORE POWER RANGERS THERE WAS...
SUPER SENTAI
Himitsu Sentai GORENGER
THE CLASSIC MANGA BY SHOTARO ISHINOMORI

FAILURE FRAME
I BECAME THE STRONGEST AND ANNIHILATED EVERYTHING WITH LOW-LEVEL SPELLS
Story by KAORI SHINOZAKI
Art by SHO
Character Designs by KWKM

Superwomen IN LOVE!
HONEY-TRAP & RAPID RABBIT
STORY & ART BY sometime

DAI DARK
STORY & ART BY Q HAYASHIDA

SEVENSEASENTERTAINMENT.COM
Visit and follow us on Twitter at twitter.com/gomanga/

Seven Seas